THE MURDER

OF

DON GIOVANNI

Ossia: What Happens in Prague Stays in Prague

BY

SUSAN LARSON

SAVVY PRESS

Library of Congress Control Number: 2025939128

ISBN: 9781939113825 Trade Paperback
ISBN: 9781939113832   Kindle

Savvy Press
481 Beattie Hollow Rd
Salem NY 12865
www.savvypress.com
info@savvypress.com

Cover: The Estates Theatre House, Prague, Czeehia

Printed in the United States of America

For BooBoo and Pop

Foreword and Backword

Were you and I, dear reader, to climb aboard a coach with Mozart in 1787 and travel from Vienna to Prague, the trip would take us three days. We would stop every 20 miles or so, to change out weary horses for fresh ones, and to give our battered bottoms some relief from the punishment they have received from the jolts and lurches of our vehicle. Steel-spring shock absorbers would have just become available in coaches, but—too bad—our vehicle doesn't have them.

We might take some refreshment, perhaps standing up (see above): either snacks we have prudently brought along, or whatever refreshment is on offer at staging posts and inns along the way. We would sleep two nights in roadside guesthouses, with or without fleas or bedbugs; in towns like Moravské Budějovice in Moravia, only 73 miles from Vienna; and in places like Němečky Brod, 80 miles from Prague.

Němečky Brod is Czech for "German Ford," which means there's a river to cross, but no bridge to cross it on. Our horses and vehicle would be wallowing across a more or less shallow portion of a stream in which we may get dunked, or maybe only drenched and splattered with mud. Thank heaven we have brought along some bottles of wine to help us remain in good humor. Besides, we are travelling with Mozart, who is a non-stop entertainer: telling jokes, making up riddles and games, improvising poetry, and inventing goofy nicknames for his fellow-travelers.

In the year 1787, the Mozarts—Wolfgang and his beloved wife Constanze—traveled from Vienna to Prague and back twice: once in January and once again in October. On their first trip, a large posse of their friends (and their dog Gaukerl) accompanied them, taking up two entire coaches; and a merry, raucous bunch they would have been despite the cold, rain, snow, ice, muck, and potholes on the roads. The composer had been invited to Prague to participate in a series of three gala concerts in the gorgeous new Nostic National Theater. He was already a superstar in that city because the theater had produced his great operas, *The Abduction from the Seraglio* and *The Marriage of Figaro*, to wild acclaim. Now at long last, Mozart himself was paying his fans an in-person visit!

The evening after his arrival Mozart would play a solo clavier recital (including a half-hour of improvised variations on the Praguers' all-time favorite tune "Non più andrai" from *Figaro*). The next night he would conduct a performance of that beloved opera in its entirety, and on the final evening of his visit he would attend the world premiere of his D Major symphony, commissioned by the city of Prague and played by the city's orchestra, conducted by the distinguished Maestro Johann Joseph Strobach.

The whole town went berserk, of course! Who would not have braved any discomforts to attend these concerts? Nothing like those three brilliant evenings had ever been experienced in Prague, or anywhere, or quite possibly ever!

The entire population, already in love with Mozart, was whipped into a frenzy of adoration. Their sophisticated understanding of his music moved the composer deeply. In Vienna he was seen as one of many pleasant tunesmiths, but in Prague? He was valued as highly as he thought he deserved to be.

In a spare hour between all the celebratory dinners, parties, receptions, grand balls, billiards and card games that Mozart attended, he signed a contract with Pasquale Bondini, director of the opera troupe, to write a brand-new music drama for Prague. The work was to be based on the ever-popular Don Juan story and presented in the coming season. After this fabulous and ego-boosting sojourn, Mozart took his wife and dog and friends home to Vienna and began composing *Don Giovanni*.

Mozart's second journey to Prague, to oversee the final weeks of rehearsals for his new opera and to conduct the premiere, was a more subdued affair. One coach, one wife, no posse, no dog. No pay yet for his "Prague" symphony, no advances for *Don Giovanni*. Wolfgang and Constanze were drowning in debt and had retrenched, moving from their large apartment in the center of Vienna to humbler lodgings. They were borrowing money from friends to repay other friends.

Mozart's father Leopold had died in Salzurg in May, and the composer, having had a complicated relationship with his Papa and being busy writing his opera, did not attend the funeral. Nor did he visibly give himself over to grief.

However, he was most anxious to hear news about any bequest Papa may have left him—a legacy that might ease his and Constanze's financial distress.

Even the Bohemians seemed to be practicing economies; this time the Mozarts were to be housed, not in the posh palace apartments of their January visit, but in a modest inn called The Three Lions.

But! They were returning to Prague! Praha! Prag! That glorious jewel of a city bisected by the Vltava river, dominated by its enormous and ancient Castle, enlivened by its spacious squares, graced by its gorgeous modern theater, and enriched by its many taverns, restaurants, and dance halls serving up the best food, the best beer, and the most dithyrambic balls in Central Europe! Best of all, Wolfgang was the toast of the town, and drinks were always on the house!

There are lots of more-or-less true stories about what the Mozarts did in their adopted city that October. Many of these tales seem to involve locking the composer up and ordering him to write some music. I have expanded on this theme in my story, which is as true as many of the others. Here it is.

The Three Lions Inn

October 4 and 5

E aperto a tutti quanti, viva la libertà

Wolfgang and Constanze arrive at their lodging in the evening, exhausted, dusty, bum-bruised and travel-stained; but happy to be in this friendly city once more. They take a light dinner and some good beer and retire to their rooms on the second floor.

The next morning Wolfgang, having refreshed himself by staying up all night revising certain passages of the grand finale of his new opera, descends from his rooms at The Three Lions. He has just received a note that Pascquale Bondini's little Italian opera troupe, the same troupe that introduced the city to *The Marriage of Figaro* (or The Crazy Day, as Praguers like to call it) only nine months past, is waiting for him downstairs in the common room. The *Figaro* cast are eager to greet their darling and assure him they are up to the task of performing *Don Giovanni: or The Dissolute Man Punished*. They have found this new opera to be stranger, darker, more shocking, and much more difficult than *Figaro*, but they've been working hard to learn it between their other performances and rehearsals.

The little band shrieks with delight as Mozart enters the room; they crowd around him, the men shaking his hand, the women petting him as if he were still a child and not a grown man of 31 at the height of his power. Some sing snippets from *Figaro*, some emit those high-volume laughs that singers like to cultivate.

"Signor Bondini," says Mozart, "how wonderful to see you again! And Madame Bondini, my sweet Susanna, are you ready to sing Zerlina? Panziani, my dear Figaro, get ready to play another cheeky servant! Madame Saporiti, Madame Micelli, my Countess and Cherubino, how are you both? And can it be? Yes! I see that we are honored by a visit from our patron of all patrons, his

Excellency Count Nostic himself!"

Count Franz Anton von Nostic, the builder and owner of the Count Nostic National Theater, The Supreme Count of the Castle, head of the Gubernium—not to mention the heroic Commander (Ret.) of all the Prague armed forces—parts the crowd of his employees, and addresses the composer with a click of his heels and a voice of command,

"Mozart! *Vitetjte zpět v Praze! Wilkommen zurück in Prag!* Welcome back to Prague! We await your getting down to business and running a sing-through after this hopefully brief celebration. I understand that the overture has not yet been written!"

Mozart sweeps Count Nostic an extravagant bow, as is proper for the employee of Prague's most illustrious citizen and patron of the arts.

"Lovely to see you once again, dear Count. As to the overture, I've been toiling away on it all night and it's almost completed. The ink will be dry by tomorrow for certain and ready for your copyists to make the parts. You may have absolute confidence in me."

The Count nods briskly, swivels in a crisp military about-face, and leaves the Inn, brushing shoulders with an elderly, very tall and swarthy man who is just entering.

"Ah, and here he is!" cries Bondini, "Our dear Signor Casanova, the famous traveler and escape artist, just arrived from Dux, in the countryside. He so wants to make your acquaintance Signor Mozart! He's heard so much about you from your mutual friend, Signor Da Ponte. Casanova is a musician and a writer also!"

"Yes, indeed," says that gentleman, taking stage and addressing the whole room. "As a matter of fact, I am come to town to oversee the publication of my novel of an entirely new genre; I call it 'science fiction.' I am also releasing a modest pamphlet describing my death-defying escape. And, of course, to hear the newest work of by the master of *The Seraglio* and *Figaro*."

"Casanova loves the theater," says Bondini. "Especially opera. He's been hanging around rehearsals amusing us all with wild tales of his adventures. He hopes you will allow him to attend rehearsals of *Don Giovanni*, whose amorous exploits compare with his own, or so he tells our young ladies."

Mozart is vaguely annoyed at Casanova's rudeness in trumpeting his own accomplishments before greeting him, as politeness demands.

"I am pleased to meet a friend of my friend Da Ponte, Signor."

"So!" says Casanova, further neglecting the formalities and squinting at the composer from his great height, "This is Signor The Towering Genius Mozart! I must say, forgive my frankness, that he is not at all what I expected."

"And what did you expect, Signor?" says Mozart.

"Well, I pictured you as a more imposing a presence, if you know what I mean."

"You mean, something along the lines of the dashing Chevalier de Saint-George of Paris, or someone who merely Towers, as do you, over the common run of men? Is that your problem?" says Mozart.

Casanova backs off a few paces and makes a conciliatory gesture, but he is too late. Mozart has struck a balletic pose and begun to sing. The inn's little orchestra, which has been playing Figaro's greatest hit tunes in their alcove all morning, is once again noodling away at the greatest hit of all, "Non più andrai." Mozart joins in, improvising lyrics as he goes:

> *Oh, the man says he loves my composing!*
> *And he's dying to make my acquaintance.*
> *When he sees that I'm less than imposing,*
> *He informs me in case I don't know.*
> *When he sees that I'm less than imposing,*
> *He informs me in case I don't know.*

> *I'm so short I resemble a pygmy!*
> *Pocky face, lumpy nose, pudgy tummy!*
> *If you want to remove yourself from me,*
> *Kiss my ass, Casanova, and go!*
> *Kiss my ass, Casanova, and go!*

The harpist, then the flautist and the trumpet player begin to add extra flourishes of their own invention to the tune. Mozart continues singing and strutting up and down, pointing out his deficient anatomical features to the assembled company, who are now doubled over with suppressed laughter;

finally, he marches up to Casanova, spins around, flips up his coattails, and presents his behind to be kissed.

Casanova laughs uneasily and raises his hands in surrender and apology. The tall man and the short one finally bow to one another in a stiffly correct manner, shake hands, and secretly vow to hate each other forever.

"Well, well," says Bondini, "all's forgiven, friends again, so why don't we just calm down and have a nice drink and a snack?" The troupe settles onto benches at a long table. Beer, wine and punch, and succulent little Bohemian snacks are served up.

After draining his glass of punch at one go, Mozart turns to Casanova with a sweetly malign grin.

"*Allora*, Signor Casanova, tell me please, why are you renowned as an escape artist? From what dire predicaments have you escaped?"

"Ah, so many. Allow me to present you with a copy of my pamphlet when it is printed. But, since you ask.... My most famous escape took place in 1755. I was imprisoned in Venice...."

"On what charges?"

"Blasphemy. Card-sharping. Whatever. I was incarcerated in the Doge's Palace for over a year in a solitary cell under the piombe, the lead plates of the roof. You cannot imagine how hot it gets in there. Nobody escapes from that prison, but still I contrived to do it. I won't bore you with the whole tale now, for it's quite long and full of blood-curdling detail; and the troupe have already heard it several times.

"But, speaking of crimes and escapes, I understand from Da Ponte that a high Court official was murdered in the Burgtheater during a performance of your stupendous *Figaro*, and that the culprit got away and the case has never been solved. Such a scandal for you! Do you have any insights or suspicions about who might have killed the man? I heard it was a cabal of renegade Freemasons."

"Actually, all the evidence points to me," purrs Mozart, "but I will deny it, even under torture."

General laughter among the troupe, during which Casanova continue to stare at Mozart in an interrogative way, eyebrows raised.

"In truth," says Mozart, "the Imperial Censor, for it was he who died, committed suicide after a bad turn in his fortunes. The poor man's body was found in the theater, yes, but not during our run, and before onstage rehearsals had even begun. It was very upsetting to everyone. And that's all I know about it."

"My dear Signor Mozart, how dare you deprive me of a juicy tale of mayhem and murder? 'Death rings down the curtain!' 'The Murder in *Figaro*!' It's too dramatic! I insist that you produce the murdered corpse and the culprit for my delectation."

"I really would rather…but can this be our handsome Signor Bassi, Count Almaviva that was, and *Don Giovanni* that will be, coming late to the party?"

"Ah, Signor Mozart," says Bondini, "Bassi's chronically late! Perhaps he woke up late after an assignation 'under the pines in the little grove,' eh? Or perhaps he just wants to make a dramatic solo entrance. Bassi will cut a fine figure as the Don, will he not?"

"Definitely pleased to be seeing you and singing your music again, Maestro," says the handsome and very young man, bowing, blushing prettily and flashing his shining white teeth. "I have been practicing my three little airs as well as the ensembles. But I'm on fire to see my big solo *scena* and put it into my voice."

"Delighted as always, dear Signor Bassi. About the big solo *scena*…well, you see, life has been hectic and, I, ah, just began working on it last night. Would you like to see what I have so far? I'll go get the short score for you!"

Mozart springs up and runs out of the common room. In a few minutes he re-appears, in an evident state of distress; gasping, eyes a-bulge, gesturing wildly and shrieking at the top of his lungs:

"Oh terrible! Horrible! Help! Come quick! There's a dead body in my room! Oh God have mercy!" He pirouettes and staggers back down the hall.

As one, the little troupe rises and stampedes after the composer, followed by the orchestra, the bartender, the patrons and the wait-staff, all thundering down the hall, up the stairs and down the upper hallway, uttering cries of horror and delight. They crowd into an open doorway and stick there, yowling and shoving, until Casanova elbows his way through them, shouting "I'm a physician! Stand aside!"

He bursts free of the knot of artistes, tipplers, and barmaids who are sucked into the room in his wake.

There, on the Turkey carpet next to a writing table, is the body of a woman, her face pale, one arm thrown over her head, the other lying limp on the coverlet which conceals the rest of her from the onlookers.

Casanova straddles the woman, unlacing her bodice; he yanks it down along with her shift and plunges his ear between her exposed breasts.

"AAAH! Get off me, you smelly old goat! What the hell are you doing?" yells the corpse, who wriggles and writhes out from under Casanova, dives under the table and wraps the coverlet around her bosom. "Who the fuck are you and who are all these people, anyway?"

"Dear Madame," says Casanova, rising to his knees, "I beg you please to pardon me, but that gentleman over there told us you were dead, and we all came to see if you were. Your heartbeat...."

"Which gentleman? Do you mean that one leaning against the door laughing his ass off at you all? The one who likes to prank innocent people with his infuriating practical jokes? That one?"

"Madame, that gentleman happens to be the famous composer Mozart."

"He happens to be my husband, you nitwit. I'm his wife."

"But then, why did he tell us all that you were dead on the floor?"

"Asleep! I was *asleep* on the floor, couldn't you tell? Stop looking so stupid. See here. We stayed up all night last night. The famous composer Mozart was working on the finale of his new opera, and I set some cushions on the floor close to his desk and was lying on the rug reading to him from "The Thousand and One Nights" to help keep him awake, like Scheherazade did, you know. Then at dawn I must have...."

"Now, there's a nice lively talking corpse for all you ghouls!" giggles Mozart. "This came off ever so much better than I had hoped! That'll teach you to pester me for tales of murder and mayhem! Are you really a physician, *Dottore* Casanova? Can't you even tell the living from the dead?"

"A medical man first listens for a heartbeat, however faint. And that is what I did, sir."

"Right. And copped a free feel off my wife in the process, didn't you? Wasn't that a good joke? I thought of my beloved, catching up on her sleep on the carpet among her cushions, when you started talking about murder and corpses, and I said to myself, wouldn't it be funny if…and Goddamn, it was! Now my darling, get up, put yourself back together, make Casanova apologize for groping you, and I'll escort you downstairs for the second half of the party."

"But Maestro!" shouts Bassi, pouting and knitting his brow, "Where's my big solo *scena*?"

"Oh, there isn't one," chirps Mozart. "I just needed an excuse to leave the room. You'll have to make do with the other three."

The crowd, in various stages of disappointment and titillation, makes for the door. Bassi doesn't budge. He pouts and gazes at the floor for a minute, then turns abruptly and stomps out.

Constanze Mozart, lately a corpse, laces up her bodice and observes,

"You know you're being a jerk."

"I can't help it. It's my nature. The troupe were so glad to see me again; they were fawning on me and petting me. Even old Nostic was semi-civil, and the house band was playing my music, and the servers were bowing to me as if I were a lord. Then that blowhard Casanova started insulting my looks and quizzing me about Hägelin's death in the theater! He acted as if he knew that I knew about it, which God knows I do. I felt I had to do something."

"And so you did something. How very uninhibited of you. Rather like Don Giovanni."

"Touché, my dear. It's true, all this Prague love goes to my head and makes me feel godlike, and quick to anger when I am scorned. I am much better behaved in Vienna where there is a King Emperor, a royal court and courtly etiquette, and where the exalted beings there regard me as a piano teacher instead of a deity."

"I can remember a few pranks you pulled in Vienna, too."

"All right, all right. Bless me for I have sinned. Henceforth I'll apply both bit and curb, collect myself, and play the mortal notesmith."

"Speaking of notesmithing, what's this about making a grand *scena* for the ridiculously handsome Bassi?"

"I lied about it as part of the joke, I'm afraid. I can't see Don Giovanni having a big soul-baring scene all to himself. For one thing, he's got a tiny shriveled soul, and for two things, he can't bear being alone. I suppose thing one follows thing two…."

"Well, I predict Signor Adonis Giovanni is not going to take his lack of a big solo turn any too well. He made such a pretty *moue*. Now I want you to come along and be a good boy and drink a toast to the success of the Don and everybody concerned with his success. I'll water my wine, because Mama says it's best not to drink too heavily during a pregnancy. Besides, I feel the need to stay alert so as to prevent any more shenanigans from you."

The Party Continues

Il padre? Lascia, o cara, la rimembranza amara!

Mozart and his wife rejoin the gathering in the common room. There is an embarrassed silence. The orchestra plays "Non più andrai" again.

"So-o-, Maestro, how are you enjoying Prague?" says Signora Saporitti.

"Ever so well, considering that I haven't left the inn yet. But I recall that everybody loves my music and everybody wants to buy me a drink and stuff me with wonderful food, and dance German dances with me, so what more could I ask?"

"Lorenzo, I mean, you know, Signor Da Ponte," continues Saporitti, "when he was here for the Lenten Balls last spring, whispered in my ear that he never sees you so happy as when you visit Bohemia."

"He is, of course lying, as a poet does and as a poet must; and Lorenzo must, more than most poets must. Here's the truth; until I arrived in Prague for *Figaro* I had *never* been happy in Bohemia before. But! That's not to say I had not travelled here. I visited Bohemia about twenty years ago, for the purpose of dying of the smallpox."

"Oooh, and did you die?" giggles Signora Micelli.

"I tried my best, my dear, and my dear Papa did all he possibly could to help me expire, but alas, I could not do it. Although the scars you see on either side of my enormous and turnip-like nose have made me even uglier than the Good God had originally intended."

"We all think you're gorgeous, don't we, boys and girls?" says Madame Bondini. "But tell us how you came here that first time. Were you on tour?"

"In a way. My father, my sister and I were in Vienna for the big wedding of one of the Empress's daughters—I don't remember which—all princesses begin to look alike after a time. My father was certain we could catch the royals in an expansive mood and win some patronage, or a gig, or some small coins, or a few more snuffboxes, or perhaps a promise of any of these.

"Anyway, the bride died in the smallpox epidemic which happened to be raging when we arrived and continued to rage while we were there. Papa said we must not flee the city, brave young artists that we were, because he had heard a rumor that our beloved co-Emperor Joseph, long may he reign, might have mentioned our names at court.

"While awaiting a possible summons to the Imperial presence, I caught the dread disease. What to do? Papa packed up my sister and me, crammed us into a carriage and headed North. We jounced around for what could have been weeks until we arrived, somehow still clinging to life, in Brno, where Nannerl also caught smallpox; and where Papa swiftly made arrangements for me to perform for some nobleman or other there. Of course, need you ask, I was eager and willing! The show must go on, be the child healthy, contagious, delirious with smallpox, or even dead! Let no one say I don't know my filial duty and my obligations as a servant of the Muses!

"But, woe is me, the concert was cancelled, and we fled again to a remote Bohemian village, I seem to have forgotten its name, where somebody took us in, and where I tried my very best to expire; I raved in a fever and tore the sheets, went stone blind for two weeks. I was thus useless for any concert Papa might arrange, for at least a month. There actually were concerts, but Nannerl filled in for me. She was sick too, but with a milder case. Plus, she was and is, a better keyboard player than I am. I don't remember much of Bohemia from that junket, having missed the concerts. And the sightseeing."

"Is your father remorseful that he used you in such a heartless manner?"

"He may well be; it is not for us mortals to know, since he is dead since this May."

"Did you not attend his deathbed and reconcile with him?"

"No, I was too busy with work to make the journey to Salzburg. I missed the funeral too. You can imagine the state I was in. Or can you? My sister had to sub for me again."

"Oh, how very sad."

"To be sure. However, some of my friends and I did get up a little proxy funeral in Vienna, with a few select mourners. My whistling starling had passed away about the same time as my father did; he could sing all sorts of tunes. My starling, I mean, not my father. Being inconsolable at his passing, I arranged a little burial ceremony, to commemorate his life in art. I wrote a poem for him and the invitees all wore veils and feathers and black gloves. We sang some hymns and solemnly buried him under a flower pot in the garden. It was a lovely service. It was very cathartic for me."

Beat. Constanze catches her husband's eye and glowers.

Beat. Even the orchestra is silent.

"Well, well, my chickens, we may as well, ah...." stammers Bondini, "All troop over to the theater and have that sing-through, don't you think? I'll join you shortly, for I see our host beckoning to me in an urgent way. Probably wants some cash in advance for your room and board. Shoo now, my darlings, it's time to show Signor Mozart your best singing."

About Josepha Dušek

Who is Josepha Dušek? What is she, that all our swains commend her, and why is she about to make an appearance in this story? She, dear reader, is the grand diva assoluta of Central Europe, and the more powerful half of Bohemia's musical Power Couple (the other half being the noted pianist, composer and teacher, her husband and mentor František Dušek)?

Who is Josefína Dušková, née Josepha Hambacher, born in Prague and the toast of of that city, Vienna, Dresden, Weimar, Leipzig, Warsaw and Berlin?

Who is as kind as she is fair, and possessed with a stunningly lovely voice of great power, range and expressiveness?

For whom Mozart has already written one bravura concert air, and, during the course of this tale will write another? And later, her future friend and admirer Beethoven will write yet a third?

With whom Mozart may have had a youthful flinglet?

Who, being independently wealthy, has never signed an opera company contract, remaining a independent free-lance concert artist? Then to Josepha let us sing. The diva is about to make her entrance.

Constanze and Josepha Dušek do Lunch

October 6, 1787

Si eccelente è'l vostro cuoco, che lo volli anch'io provar

Prague awakes to another crisp, sunny autumn morning. Constanze Mozart has spent the previous day doing necessary domestic tasks: unpacking, setting their quarters to rights, mending some travel-torn garments. These wifely duties she alternates with short naps and writing letters to her mother, sisters, and son. She is already bored.

Today however, she is pleasantly surprised to receive three letters. One is from the illustrious soprano Josepha Dušek, just returned from a concert tour, inviting her to lunch the next day at a nearby restaurant.

Constanze, remembering the whispers about Dušek and Wolfgang— however long-over and however long-before the Weber girls had come to his attention—feels her hackles rise in a spasm of jealousy. Lunch with her husband's former flame? Ugh!

On the other hand.… A rich, and solidly-married friend of Wolfgang's, and a generous *saloniste* whose doors and purse were always open to artists less fortunate than herself? Mrs. Mozart makes the effort to smooth her hackles back down, calculating that the Grand Diva Dušek might be persuaded to help them financially in their time of trouble. So, lunch.

The other two letters, from certain men she has only just met, offer her a promise of amusement in Prague. She is flattered and delighted that somebody is paying her some attention as an actual female person and not just an appendage on the Towering Genius. Especially the younger and handsomer of the certain men.

The two women meet at a famous restaurant in the Old City and are shown to the *Stammtisch*, the artist's reserved table, and settle themselves in for a serious luncheon.

"What would you like, Frau Mozart? The wild game here is superb, and the fish is fresh from the fishmonger's barrel. My treat."

"Oh, my, many thanks; let me see. I'll have the trout. And the pheasant confit. Some bread and cheese and the wild mushrooms in cream sauce, and perhaps some picked cabbage and a fruit tart...."

"My dear, such an appetite! Forgive me for being nosy, but are you...."

"Pregnant? Yes indeed. I am praying hard that this one will live. We just lost a little son recently, and we have only the one at home, staying with his grandmamma. I would so love another child. So would Wolfgang."

"I pray for your success. Take good care of yourself! No excitement! Eat whatever you want! So. What's it like being married to the Great Man?"

"About my marriage to a celebrity; I was about to ask you the same question."

"To be sure, my situation is different. I married my music teacher, he's much older; he's more like my father. Besides, all modesty aside, I have managed to become much more famous than he is. Oh, I beg your pardon, no offense intended...."

"None taken. That's not my situation; you're right. My sisters are famous, and I am not. I have some skill as a singer, but not the temperament. I'm really more the domestic type. I like keeping house and doing the accounts, which is no easy task because Wolfgang is so careless with money. I love looking after my sweet Carl, going out with my sisters, and organizing dinner parties for all our friends. That's all I need to be happy and busy. My life here in Prague, please excuse me, where I sit in the corner in the dance houses or sit in my room incubating and darning my stockings, is probably going to be really boring. Annoying. Enraging, at times, being married to the great man. Oh my dear God in heaven, this pheasant is absolutely delicious!"

"And aside from eating your way through the city, have you yet no plan to amuse yourself while the troupe and Wolfgang rehearse *Don Giovanni* and carouse after hours?"

"Well, some opportunities have arisen, actually, and I'd love your advice: I got a letter yesterday; it's an invitation from, ah, one of the singers in the troupe. He has asked to be my tour guide and show me all the sights, during those hours when he is not called at the theater."

"Ah…The ambrosial Signor Bassi. How sweet."

"How did you know it was Bassi?"

"He's the only single man in the company."

"Oh. Walking about with him wouldn't appear too scandalous, would it? I am an old married woman of 25 and he is scarcely out of boyhood."

"Exactly Like the Countess and Cherubino, don't you think? Tongues may wag. Just as they wag about the love I bear your husband."

"What sort of love might that be, exactly?"

"Oh, calm yourself, my dear. It's purely professional. I adore him of course, but who does not in this town? He is an adorable sprite! His music is sublime, and I love singing that aria he wrote just for me ten years ago. But you know I have a lover, yes? My patron, the handsome and gifted Count Clam-Gallas. And I have another casual affair going as well. So let's not harbor suspicions and be so prickly with one another; let's be friends and allies."

"All right. Friends and allies. But what about your husband?"

"Well, he is rather old. Besides, he has always preferred men. We have an understanding."

"Why did you marry him?"

"Oh, I love him certainly, deeply and to this day. He was my teacher and is now my colleague also. We have made so much wonderful music together, and we tell each other the naked truth in everything. My father objected to our marriage of course, because František is the son of a robot from the countryside; even though he is highly educated."

"Son of a what?"

"A robot. It's the Czech word for work, or a peasant who is forced to do unpaid labor for his lord. A serf. Or a slave, you could say.

"Anyhow František had a patron who recognized his talent—a nobleman who was also his first lover, and who sponsored his musical studies in Vienna. I insisted on marrying František because he was my idol, my hero; he opened the world of music to me. He nurtured my talents and presented me to the public when I was ready. I told Papa firmly, that when we went on concert tours together, as we had begun to, it would be convenient if we were a married couple."

"You are so very frank with me! I can see you are someone who needs to tell the naked truth to everyone, not just your husband. I admire you for being so forthright, and I promise I will return the favor. Who is your new love interest then?"

"Would you believe it's the decrepit Venetian? Casanova. He heard me in a recital a while back, on one of his many trips to town, and has been pestering me ever since."

"Ugh! I mean, pardon me, I can't quite see the charm."

"Well, he has a brilliant and cultivated mind; he's met the Emperor and the Pope and the King of Prussia. He's led a life chock full of adventure; *the tales* he tells! And the—between you and me, certain rumors have reached even the provincial capital of Prague; rumors suggesting that he is a master of the art of love. I wanted to find out what all the fuss was about. So I found out."

"And the verdict?"

"It's true. He is no longer virile, but he has the knack of making me feel as if I were the only woman in the world, ever. He looks, touches, tastes with an incredible delicacy combined with the greedy ecstasy of a young lover; and he has more ways of making a woman come that I can count. So yes, he is master of all the amatory arts that still remain to him. The rumors don't tell the half of it. Are you interested?"

"I received a letter from him too, just this morning."

"Did you then?"

"Now *you* calm yourself, Madame. It's just a lovely letter of contrition and apology. Our first meeting was extremely unpleasant, and until I got this note I thought him to be sovereignly odious."

"I'm sure you did. But it's your husband who is to blame for that little caper, not Casanova."

"I have spoken to him."

"And Casanova really is something of a medical man, after all. He saved the life of a Venetian Senator when all the doctors had failed. Or so he claims."

"Since we are being so frank with each other, I'll read you his letter. You will see how sincere and repentant he is."

Here Constanze, her rosy cheeks darkening to crimson, slips her hand through her pocket hole, takes a folded paper from her purse, unfolds and smooths it against her breast, and reads:

Dearest Madame, (I can't believe I'm reading this to you!)

> *In re our abrupt and shocking meeting yesterday, I wish to assure you of my most profound distress at frightening you so badly. I revere all womankind and would never lift a violent hand in the direction of the fair sex, of which you are certainly a shiningly lovely example, even wrapt in the arms of Morpheus and sprawled on the carpet. I beg you, I implore you, to forgive me my impulsiveness. I have some medical skill and no little knowledge of reviving the dead or near-dead, which I had been—falsely!— given to believe was your condition. I once saved the life of a Venetian Senator in that city, when all the doctors had failed. This Senator became my grateful lifelong benefactor thereafter. No harm, no harm in the world, was meant you, dearest and loveliest of ladies. Please be so merciful as to accept my most abject apologies, and permit me to call upon you, that I might bend my knee before you and offer myself to you as your adoring slave.*

> *With greatest regards, admiration, etc. etc.,*
> *Giacomo Casanova, Chevalier de Seingnalt*

"Ah, trotting out the very same Venetian story, and buttering you up at the same time, the old rogue! He knows how to get round a woman and ease himself into her good graces, and other places as well."

"You think he is not sincere?"

"I doubt that even *he* knows when he is not sincere. Conning, scamming, and cheating at cards is his stated profession. Living a voluptuary's life is his credo. But be warned, I hear that he is also quick to avenge any offense, real or imagined, to his dignity. They say that your dear man got the better of him, not once but twice, at the Three Lions. Perhaps Casanova thinks to even that score by seducing the lonely wife while the husband toils day and night in the theater...."

"Or plays billiards and cards in the taverns. Hmm. 'And there was light'.... You are most certainly right about this. The old man makes love to me to get back at Wolfgang! Damn Men! The nasty stupid games they play on us! I hate them all so much right now, even my husband! Wolfgang is always after me to behave more modestly and avoid any hint of scandal, while he…All this Enlightenment and Free-thinking fad has just given men free rein to behave worse than *ever*!

"Perhaps an affair with the old goat might be a nice revenge for you, then! He won't get you pregnant; that's doubly guaranteed. Listen my dear, why should the Enlightenment be only for the men? Why can't women be libertines too, and take our pleasure where we find it?"

"Something to do with being left with the baby, perhaps?"

"But why is wantonness the exclusive property of the Empress of Russia and forbidden to the rest of womankind?"

"Excepting the Empress, I would say that Custom, the Law, and the Church do not tilt in our sex's favor."

"These Da Pontes and Beaumarchais and Casanovas and noblemen fucking their way across Europe, slithering around actresses and singers and servant girls, all the while expecting their own women to guard their chastity! It's not *fair*!

"Listen, Constanze, I have an idea. Why don't we play a game with these two admirers? Why not behave however we like with them? Flirt, lead them on, deny them, bed them, spurn them, bed them again? We could even trade off on alternate days, you with the old man, and I with the boy. Just for fun of course.…"

"I…don't know.… I don't want to be the guilty one if there is an imbroglio. But what imbroglio could happen if we take precautions? A little fun, a little joke, a smidge of revenge! We could really entertain ourselves! Let's do it!"

"Agreed! Let's write them some letters of encouragement, shall we?"

"Before we do that, I am panting to ask you, Madame Dušek, with all your brio and boldness, why is it that you have never appeared in opera?"

"Ah, well. My father forbade me."

"Wolfgang's father forbade him to marry me, but he did it anyway."

"I love my Papa dearly, and I felt I was in no position to defy him again after marrying a low-born man. Although when I look at roles like the Countess or Konstanze, it really makes me sorry. Papa is a bourgeois of no rank; he's just a shopkeeper. He views are so conservative; in his opinion, actresses and opera singers are all whores. He didn't want me to associate with such base people. Sadly, he isn't entirely wrong. Some of the girls in the

National Theater have little side businesses going with certain patrons, to make ends meet. Even if they marry within the troupes to double their wages and halve their rent, I believe they still might work out an accommodation with the right count or baron or wealthy merchant. Necessity dictates, I'm afraid. The way of the world."

"I am aware."

"Dear Papa didn't need to protect me from selling myself; we are quite wealthy. But he made me promise never to soil our reputation as a respectable family by going on the opera stage and painting and wigging and dressing up as somebody else in front of the public. So, reluctantly, I vowed to him I never would. To this day I honor him by singing only concerts and recitals."

"But...."

"Yes, I know, I have a longtime lover, but that's different. I chose him of my own free will. Count Clam-Gallas is a nobleman, a longtime friend of František's family, and a musical colleague. He provides me with the regular sexual pleasure that my husband cannot give. So you see. My father, the old dear, defers to Clam-Gallas's noble rank and pretends ignorance of our arrangement. You must come out to have dinner and meet them all, very soon."

"But! Another question! About the painting and wigging? I'm so confused about who is who here and what is acceptable behavior and what is seen as scandalous. All the fine ladies in Prague dress so—so colorfully; and they make up just like actresses or like the- the street girls in Vienna. Sometimes I can't tell the respectable women from, you know…"

"Ah, the clown paint! The gobs of whiteface, the blots of rouge, the fake moleskin eyebrows, the carmined lips, the swarms of beauty patches. Do we look too grotesque and ridiculous? Isn't this sort of makeup still the fashion in the west of Europe?"

"The noble and rich ladies still use the white make-up in Vienna, and I think in Paris, but I think they use just a little bit less...."

"I suppose we look to you like a troupe of circus performers ten years out of fashion! Prague was great once, but now it's only a provincial backwater; we have no royal court anymore. We women are so terribly insecure about not being á la mode, so we tend to overdo everything. I'm so used to it, onstage and off, that I don't think about it; but our fashion sense must seem so odd to people from the great capitals, like you. although I detect a whisper of rouge and discreetly blackened brows now that I look at you."

"Yes, It's my own homemade rouge and a little burnt cork."

"But I think you look lovely, my dear. The fresh glow of expectant motherhood, so chaste and modest…oh heavens, I'm sorry, now I'm saying man-things!"

"That's all right. I am neither lady nor a whore, just a plain housewife of the artisan class. Have I mentioned how delicious this food is?

"Dear Papa doesn't seem to notice how garish we Praguesses look, because if the nobles are painting masks onto their faces, we must ape them. Besides! I am a walking advertisement for him! Do you know who compounds all the high-end makeup in the region? The White Unicorn! Papa! He grinds the powders himself, and makes them into pastes. He has made quite a fortune from it. He knows it's not really beneficial for his good ladies, but what can he do? Every woman of rank or means clamors for his great jars of *rouge et blanc*."

"Then what do the- the professional girls here do to distinguish themselves from the nobility?"

"Oh, performers have to use all use the best stuff, it reads better from the stage and it doesn't run onto your fichu and stomacher quite so badly. The prostitutes go with the cheaper paint, and much less of it. Bismuth for white, Sandalwood or wine paste for red. It runs when one sweats, so the street girls wear red or pink to hide it. If there's still any doubt about their rank in life, they just yell out their price. In this town, a woman without a thick coat of paint is likely to be considered to be of easy virtue; just be aware of that if you go out alone. Speaking of which, shall we pay the bill and write our billet-doux?"

"After dessert. Oh, what angel made this tart? We can go back to the inn and write them there."

"Too dangerous. Better here. Our host will loan you a pen, and you can write on the reverse of Bassi's note. Tell me now, what does he say?"

"Have a look."

Please permit me to show you some of the attractions in the city. If you please can you meet me for an hour before rehearsals begin tomorrow at nine? Please let me know if you will, and please select a convenient

> *meeting place.*
> *Luigi Bassi.*

"Well, he says 'please' a lot, that's nice, but his style is terrible."

"He seems very earnest and unsophisticated. I like that better than the tired clichés of other one."

"Now I will write to the other one, as a sort of go-between for you, saying you are presently engaged elsewhere, but I am still willing and you may become available later. Keep him guessing. Let me dictate your note to Bassi, though; I have more experience of intriguing than you. Let's see; (she sings, sotto voce) 'what sweet little breezes will sigh this evening....'"

"Little breezes?"…Oh nonono, haha! Bassi may be young and innocent but surely he'll remember that canzonetta!"

"Well, how about 'meet me under the *Orloj* before rehearsals, at nine thirty?'"

"The what?"

"The Clock in the Old Square. The starting point for all Prague flirtations. Now, I'll get my footman to deliver these notes, and we can stroll over to the Orloj to orient you, and then back to the Three Lions."

The two women finish their meal, and wander arm in arm, softly humming the canzonetta: "Sull'aria" from *Figaro*. They examine the ancient town clock before making their way back to the Inn.

Turning the last corner, they are met by the sight of the Mozarts' luggage being piled up outside in the street and the innkeeper supervising its removal. Constanze flies at him, yanking at his sleeve and spinning him around to face her.

"You, my host, pardon me, but what the bloody hell are you doing with our luggage?"

"I am so sorry, Madame, but there have been complaints lodged, Madame. Several patrons were very upset about the incident yesterday morning, and they have written to say they will never come here so long as the Mozarts are in residence, Madame."

"What? You're telling me that you have never had 'incidents' at an inn before? Debates? Arguments? Fistfights? Drunken brawls? Besides, the

Theater has a contract to house visiting artists here! You can't throw us out for having a bit of harmless fun! Look, I am expecting a child any minute, and I can't be traipsing all over Prague from inn to inn like the Blessed Virgin Mary, just because a few assholes lack a sense of humor! I need my goddamn rest!"

"Madame," (he gazes doubtfully at Constanze's small baby bump) "I have contacted Herr Bondini, and he will find you another lodging, and we'll move everything, including Herr Mozart's clavier, free of charge. The complaints came from people of rank, and I am helpless to ignore them, Madame."

"Who? Who complained? Give me his name!"

"I am pledged to silence, Madame. Please, Madame."

"*Du calme*, dear Constanze," says Josepha. "I have a pretty good idea who the complainant might be. Revenge, and double revenge."

"You don't think…. Oh yes, you do! Ugh! What a scoundrel, buttering me up and tossing me out all at once! You can have that mangy old satyr, or what's left of him, if you want to, but I will never speak to him again!"

"But! Why don't you come and lodge with us at Bertramka for the next two weeks? We'd love to have you, and we're only three miles away. It's peaceful there and Wolfgang can work from the clavier in the music room, and you can get some peace and quiet when you need it."

"That would be lovely, but are you sure we're not imposing?"

"Oh, no, we host any number of visiting artists; but our greatest honor would be to welcome the towering genius and his enchanting, deliciously profane wife! Besides, we can hatch our libertine plots and report back to each other, in total privacy."

"You are too good. I accept on my and my husband's account. Let me call a cart to take all this stuff I just finished unpacking."

An Afternoon Coffee Musicale at Bertramka

October 6, 1787

Ehi, caffè! Ciocolatte!

Constanze arises from her nap in an airy bedroom at the Villa Bertramka. She gazes out the window at the vista of the Vltava and the many -steepled city of Prague to the north and east of the hill upon which the villa is situated. Further up the hill are the vineyards, their branches bare after the harvest. The silence, after the bustle of the Three Lions, makes her glad.

She hums "Sull'aria" from *Figaro*, fixes her hair, adjusts the lace of her fichu, and sighs a few times in satisfaction. Their luggage has been unpacked and refreshed, and their books and scores shelved by the Bertramka staff. She has sent out two messages—one a reply to Signor Bassi, and the second to her husband at the National Theater, telling him of their unexpected move to Bertramka, but not mentioning the reason for it. She expects Mozart to arrive sooner, or maybe later.

Or maybe now! A silvery spray of clavier music floats up to her window. Constanze claps her hands in delight and heads for the music room downstairs. Entering, she sees a young man and a middle-aged one seated on the bench playing a four-hands arrangement of her husband's D major symphony, premiered in Prague a few months ago. The great conductor Strohbach, whom she has met before, is seated in an armchair, eyes closed, beating time and cueing an invisible orchestra. Madame Dušek, lounging on the divan drinking coffee, gestures for Constanze to sit by her. She does so, accepting a demitasse. She guesses that the two performers are Count Clam-Gallas and Herr Dušek, respectively. After the final cadence, there is much laughter and applause, and joyful introductions all around.

"Bravo! Well played! I love that symphony!" With that, Wolfgang A. Mozart, for it is he, bounds into the room.

Who wrote that thing, do you surmise?
The fellow right before your eyes!

He embraces Strobach and shakes the hands of the two players, saying: "Worthies! What a treat to meet you!" He kisses both his wife and Madame Dušek:

Ladies! I am charmed to greet you,
but wait, I'm sure we've met before,
now wait a moment I implore,
familiar faces, charming dames,
I just cannot recall your names!

"My dear, I'm your wife and why are you talking in rhymes?"

A mania seizes me sometimes!

"Dear Mozart, welcome at last to my house."

Danke, from me on behalf of my spouse!

"František Dušek whispers to Constanze, "does he take these fits often?""
"Only when he's in a bad mood, which isn't all that often, Herr Dušek," she whispers back. Aloud, she says,
"Dearie, if you won't stop rhyming, perhaps you could play to us a little."

Good! I'll sit and pound the keys,
while these fine people take their ease.

The composer seats himself at the keyboard, rolls a first-inversion chord, and sings:

They managed to stagger through the play

That's all that they could do today,
Such a torment of wrong notes,
Lost places and constricted throats,

The Don is harder than they knew,
They took a bite but couldn't chew.
Ow-ooooo! Hoo! Hooooo!

With that, Mozart begins to improvise on bits from the opera, adding sour notes and halting rhythms to demonstrate how the troupe butchered his music. Eventually he stops, bangs another chord and sings:

Josepha dear, a year has passed
Since I heard your aria last.
I've quite forgotten how it goes
Could you remind me, d'you suppose?

"Of course, my friend. I'm going to perform it later this evening at a house concert in Malá Strana, and I wouldn't mind a rehearsal at all."

With that, the great lady and Mozart launch themselves into "Ah, lo previdi" from memory. Constanze is awed at the power and beauty of her new friend's voice and dramatic expression, both perfectly utilized in the service of that mighty soaring piece. She is so awed in fact, that when Count Gallas requests that she and Josepha sing "Sull'aria," she agrees to do it.

Gallas seats himself at the clavier and the ladies sing in turns, quickly finding a common ground between Constanze's crystalline soprano and Josepha's golden tones. But when they begin to duet on the words *ei già il resto capirà*, both ladies crack up laughing. They stagger around whooping and holding their sides, until Mozart leaps up in annoyance:

Da capo, da capo, such shameful deporting!
Why ruin it all with your giggles and snorting!

"Oh, ho-ho-ho, we're so s-sorry! It's just that, over lunch we were making jokes about men and…and women, and…and flirtations and writing billets-doux, and then we sang this same duet over dessert:"

Well, harmless jokes don't make me jealous,
But flirting is an infidelis!

"Will you *stop* talking in rhymes please? Anyway, you men are free to flirt; why shouldn't women be, too? It does no harm if it's all in fun. Now, Josepha dear, let's take it from the top, no giggling this time."

And they do. Enchantment fills the room. The Count, deeply moved, rises from the clavier and kisses and embraces both women. Constanze kisses and embraces him back with more vim than is strictly necessary. Mozart applauds and smiles along with the rest, but he seems, at least to the one who knows him best, a bit put out.

"Good," she says to herself.

After more coffee and lively conversation, Josepha takes Mozart aside and asks him to take a short stroll with her.

On the peak of one of the hills belonging to the villa there stood a pavilion. One day the singer Frau Dušek locked up the great Mozart in a cunning way, then prepared ink, pen, and music paper and let him know that he would not be able to regain his freedom unless he composed for her the aria he promised with the words "Bella mia fiamma, addio!" Mozart yielded to necessity, but in order to avenge the prank that Frau Josepha Dušek had played on him, he introduced into the aria various passages that were difficult to perform and threatened his despotic friend that he would immediately destroy the aria if she could not perform it successfully at first sight.

Karl Mozart to Adolf Popelka, March 4, 1856

Of course, Mozart's elder son was only three years old and living with his grandmother in Vienna when this event took place, but we can be sure his report is completely accurate. Being a tactful man and protective of his famous father's reputation, he stops short of telling the whole story of what happened in the pavilion and thereafter. Now dear reader, I reveal the rest of the tale to you.

Bella Mia Fiamma

October 6 and 7, 1787

Regina, io vado ad ubbidirti!

The little party is breaking up. Constanze retires for another snooze, Clam-Gallas goes home, and František Dušek goes off to teach a lesson. Josepha finds a shawl, and she and her favorite composer exit the house into a moonlit and fragrant autumn evening.

"It's only a few paces, up the hill to my little summer house in the vineyard. You can get a nice view of Prague in the moonlight from there. And I have a little surprise for you."

Gladly, Madame, show me moon.
I'll shoot it with my musquetoon!
I love Prague in all her guises.
And you know how I love surprises.

"Oh you'll love this one, I'm sure. I am so concerned to hear the production's not coming together so well; I wish I were in the cast; I would learn your music faster than all of them and shame them into working harder. Here's the summer house. Let me unlock. Now, you must close your eyes and step inside."

"What the devil? I smell my tobacco! Have you brought my smoking things up here?"

"Yes, and some scored paper and pens and ink, and a bite of dinner and some good beer. And now dear man, you are my prisoner! Open your eyes!"

"Wait, what? Aren't you coming in, Madame? Why have you shut the door? And why the bloody hell are you locking it? It's dark as Egypt in here, even with the damned moon!"

"Candles and matches have been provided. Now that I have you under lock and key, you must obey my every wish for the rest of the evening. I demand payment for my hospitality! Write me another concert aria; I command it! Light the candles, sharpen the pens, and produce! I am not letting you out until you write me a concert piece as gorgeous as anything in Don Giovanni!"

"But Madame, this is ridiculous!! I'm supposed to be writing the damned overture! I've already written you an aria! Besides, I have no text, and even more besides, this is bloody blackmail!"

"I've sung that aria everywhere. It's ten years old and everyone's heard it at least twice. I'm singing it tonight, and after I finish, I'm giving it a rest. I need something new! If you would please light a candle and look on top of the pile of paper, you will see a text of 'Bella mia fiamma.' You remember it?"

"Vaguely...a tragical farewell aria, right?"

"That's the one. It seethes with high emotion! Perfect for me. Perfect for you. I'm not letting you out until you set it, no matter how much you beg. Now I'm going to Malá Strana to sing a little benefit concert for retired musicians, and then to a reception. That should give you plenty of time."

Woman, your heart is made of stone!
I don't have time to get this done!
Your plan is wicked, nasty, bold!
I'll stay in here until I'm old!
I won't play,
no matter what you say,
that's my position!...
Hello?...
All right, I'll do it, on one condition.

"What condition?"

If I must write it in one night,
then you must sing it off at sight.
One wrong note and I'll claim the right

to rip it into tiny bits,
do you accept or call it quits?

"I accept. I can solfège anything."

"Anything?"

"In any clef you choose. I am confident. Bye-bye now."

Mozart gropes for the table, bumps into it, and finds the candles and matches. After lighting the candle he fills his pipe and lights it, sits in the chair provided, smoking and chuckling to himself.

"What a woman! She is unstoppable, unquenchable, and unbeddable…by the likes of me anyhow. Papa, God rest him, thought she was a harridan. In other words, an opera diva. Too bad she won't take the plunge and go onstage.

"Papa liked his women servile and silent. But in my divas—a Storace, a Dušek, or Hofer, Lange, Cavalieri—I need something that's a bit too much. Or, in their cases, a lot too much. How I love them all!

"But! I'll take revenge on this harpy woman! Let's see…*my lovely flame, farewell…heaven is not disposed to render us happy…bitter death…this terrible dread, come quickly death*, and blahblahblah…all the usual opera seria cornball shit. Ah, here's beer, bread, cheese, a nice sausage as promised. Now, genius, write her a tune that no mere mortal can sight-read…good beer, by God. Really nice sausage."

For a good hour Mozart nibbles his dinner, drinks his beer, and sketches out the melody and bass of the poignant farewell: here tender, there raging, the melody leaping and plunging like a boat on the high seas. Then he gets a feeling.

"I hope the woman provided me with a chamberpot in here. Probably back in the back room, if there is a back room.…"

The genius unbuttons his breeches, grasps the candle in one hand and his member in the other, and lights his way to a door in the far corner of the room. Opening the door he sees his goal, a chamber pot glowing dully in a far corner. He makes for it, not noticing a rumpled bed next to the wall, and a duvet on the floor. Not noticing, that is, until he steps on the duvet—and what is beneath it—something which rolls softly and sickeningly beneath his foot.

He gasps. He has stood upon such yielding stuff before, in a common grave in Vienna; he recognizes it instantly. Withdrawing his foot, he bends low with the candle to confirm his knowledge…yes, it is a human hand, a man's hand. And—he bends down and takes it in his own—it is cold. He feels for a pulse. None. The owner of the hand is dead. Mozart leaps to his feet.

"*Ach du lieber Gott*! It's a corpse! And I'm peeing on it! And myself! And I've dropped the candle! And it's gone out! Help! Emergency! Somebody, anybody, help!"

With both hands now free, Mozart feels his way back along the walls to the door of the pavilion, pounds on it, first with his fists and then with his foot, shrieking above the staff all the while.

"*Zu Hilfe, zu Hilfe*! Somebody! Oh God, please, not another dead body in my life! NonononoNO! 'Sepha, come let me OUT! I'm alone in the dark with a corpse! Is there nobody on this whole estate who can hear me? Gardener, butler, washerwoman, student, wife? I'm not picky! Helphelphelp!"

Beat.

Mozart stops to think. He tucks himself back into his britches.

"All right, genius, get a grip. The household must either be drunk, asleep, or out for the evening; and you, dear little fellow, are locked in here with someone to whom you have not been introduced, and who is dead. Try the windows. Barred with wrought iron, of course. Defenestration is popular in Prague, so every precaution has been taken…

"*Fa core*, take heart, now. We have been in this situation before, teetering on a heaving sea of defunct strangers, and we survived. Remember your Masonic training. Death is a friend and not to be feared."

> *Fear not Death.*
> *Take a deep breath.*
> *Even dead, it's only flesh.*
> *Thank the gods it's fairly fresh.*
> *Now, what were we doing before the thing?*
> *Writing an air for the lady to sing.*

"*Basta*, let's apply ourselves to our assigned task. We still have the final *stretto* to complete. Let's turn our horror into a wild outburst of coloratura for our diva to negotiate—if she can. When she shows up, she's in for an even bigger surprise than the one she sprang on me.

"Brrrrr! Somebody's teeth are chattering! Let's finish the aria, and the food. But perhaps no more beer."

As the moon was sinking behind the hill, and the final bars of "Bella mia fiamma" are being written, Mozart hears footsteps on the gravel path, and a key turning in the lock. He forgets the aria and remembers the horror.

"Help! Let me out, 'Sepha! Something awful has happened! There's a dead person in here!"

"God save us, a dead person? Oh-ho-ho, now wait a moment; this is another one of your practical jokes, isn't it? Like the one you pulled at the inn? The one that got you turned out into the street? You can't use that same one again, I'm wise to you, you little scamp!"

"Nonononono, I'm not joking this time, never been so serious, come here and see, it's a man, he's dead, he's lying right here under this duvet. Look!"

"Oh all right, but.... *Oh my God, that's my father*! Is he really dead?"

"Your father? I'm afraid so, I felt for a heartbeat, and there was none. And he's ice-cold."

"Oh my dear, my beloved, my own, my dearest...." She collapses, wailing, on top of the corpse of her father. Her cries subside into a terrible silence.

"Ah, she's fainted dead away. Should I find somebody to go for a doctor? The door is open...or should I stay here with her?" He chafes her wrists, strokes her face, and loosens her shawl. "What in hell do I do now?"

Josepha comes to, clutching Mozart's coat, shoving him away from her. Eyes rolling in her head, she shrieks,

"Get away from me! I want to die too! Why did he have to die? But...who...then...covered him up with my duvet? Did *you* cover him up, Mozart?" Josepha clutches the moist duvet and pulls it off the corpse, whose face and hands glow like poison mushrooms in the pale dawn light.

"No, I didn't. I found him under it. His hand was in my path, and I stepped on it on my way to the pisspot. I was so frightened I pissed on him. Sorry."

"O how horrible! Somebody must have killed him! O dear God! Is he wounded? Did somebody stab him? Did *you* stab him?"

"Madame, I certainly did not. I have never met the man, and stabbing is not my *mode d'emploi* for introducing myself."

"There's blood...."

"It's not blood, it's...."

"This wound...."

I don't see any wound."

"He's pale as death...."

"There are no signs of struggle here that I can see. I happen to know from experience that he was not strangled. But I think we should find a doctor and. ..."

With a wailing cry Josepha lurches to her feet and runs out the door down the hill to the house. Mozart sits a while contemplating the dead man; finally he leaves the pavilion and shuts the door, slowly following in his friend's footsteps.

"She seems to have loved him."

The famous genius makes his way down through the vineyard as a rosy glow appears in the sky. He can see lamps being lit in the villa. He hears the rattle of a carriage leaving the stables and the footfalls of people running. A dark figure appears to him through the rising mists. It is Constanze. She opens her arms to her husband, wrapping his shivering body in her shawl. They stand in silence for a few minutes.

"Oh Lord have mercy, her father...how terrible, and I didn't know who it was...."

"Oh Christ have mercy I did an unforgivable thing. When she came into the house wailing and weeping, I—I laughed at her. I thought you and she were conspiring in another tasteless practical joke. Then she collapsed in front of me. I called for help and the servants carried her off to bed. I think I have lost a friend—several friends. They'll never forgive me. We'd better move back to town."

"This is what comes of my stupid pranks. I'm sorry, Stanzerl, I'm so sorry. What is happening in the house?"

"They've sent for the local doctor and the village constable. They'll be here shortly. You're still shivering. You need to warm up and have a drink of something hot before you have to speak to them. Come on into the kitchen and sit near the fire."

In less than a half-hour the local doctor arrives in the Bertramka carriage, accompanied by the constable, both fetched from the neighboring village of Smíchov. The doctor is escorted immediately to the pavilion; the constable is led into the music room where Mozart, having warmed and fortified himself in the kitchen, is waiting.

The constable is stout, middle-aged, and has evidently dressed in haste; he is wearing the tunic of his uniform over his pajamas. He shakes the composer's extended hand.

"I'm Mozart. I'm the one who discovered the body. I was locked in with it, in the little summerhouse above the vineyard."

"Constable Jiří Pospíšil. Most humbly honored, Mr. Mozart, sir. May I be so bold as to tell you that am a huge fan? I have seen both your operas, *The Abduction* and *The Crazy Day*. I mean *Figaro* but that's what we call it here, *The Crazy Day*. You know that march song you wrote, 'Non pyoo andrej?' I think it is the best music in the world. I was in the army once, sir, and I can tell you that you got it absolutely right; the slogging through the mud, the bullets whizzing by, the bad pay! It brings back the dear old days every time I hear it." The constable hums a few bars of the aria, marches in place, and bursts into tears.

"Well, thank you, officer. People here do seem to love that one. I hear it everywhere."

"And now, honored sir, I have the sad pleasure of telling you that you are detained, and you must come with me to the Police House in town, where you will be detained as a person of interest. I am sorry about that, sir, but orders is orders."

"WHAT? You must be joking!! Although I see that you are not. Nevertheless, WHAT? Twice in one day, to be put under lock and key, first by Madame, then again by YOU? Is locking up visitors to Prague some sort of a thing?"

"If it was just me, sir, I would never ever lock you up, no matter how many murders you might of did. But seeing as how you admitted to me that you were alone in a locked house all night with someone who is now dead, you are a person of interest, as we say on the force."

"But...but what if the murder happened before I arrived there, and I just found his body?"

"That's for the doctor and the coroner to say, sir, if he was murdered, who murdered him, and how, and how long the dead gentleman has been dead. In the meantime, you are in my custody. I advise you do not resist, because I may be old, but I have seen combat, and I am still pretty tough."

"What am I saying? Why did I bring up murder? What if he died by his own hand? People do that, you know."

"That's as may be, sir."

"May I at least get my hat and coat first?"

"Yes, sir, we will go together and inform your good hosts that you will be detained for a short while. A vehicle from the city is coming with detectives to examine the scene of the crime, and I will accompany you back in that same vehicle. So perhaps there is time for us to go down to the kitchen and have coffee and a little breakfast first, what do you think?"

Mozart in the Lockup, Part II

October 7, 1787

Ah! Dov'è il perfido? Dov'è l'indegno?

Tutto il mio sdegno sfogar io vo

The hero of Prague, the famous genius Mozart, has sunk into a nasty mood during the journey down from the high bluffs of the suburb of Košíře, north on the road skirting the Vltava, over the Stone Bridge, and into the Prague Central Police Station in the Old City. As he and Constable Pospíšil enter the building, the duty officers leap up in surprise and recognition. They shout his name, bowing low to him and applauding. The ruckus brings the rest of the law enforcement personnel running. The cops, guards and turnkeys take his elbows, almost lifting him off the floor, and sweep him into their cozy guardroom, where a fire is glowing in the stove. They plop him into a chair and crowd around him, shaking his hand English-style and professing in a jumbled chorus their love for him, for *The Abduction from the Seraglio* and especially *The Crazy Day*.

"You know that bit where the boy hides in the closet and then jumps out the window, so funny; or that bit where Figaro was almost going to marry his own mother, or that bit where the Count fucks his own wife but thinks it's Susanna. But really, they all agree that the best bit is where everybody—" At this point the policemen lean their heads together, break into harmony and sing: "*Ah, tutti contenti* (Ah, all of us happy) *saremo così* (we will be)."

Neither the policemen's shouted protestations of fandom, nor their mobbing him in a rough but friendly way, have moved the composer to a better emotional place. Indeed, after his own personal crazy day of disappointing rehearsals, an eviction, a sleepless evening sketching out an entire concert aria, treading and then peeing upon a dead person who turned out to be his hostess's father, being accused of murdering said dead person, being arrested and carted away to jail, and currently working on a nasty headache, he is in no mood. But hearing these voices suddenly calmed and melded in his own sublime hymn to grace, his eyes fill with tears and his mouth opens in awe.

"Oh." He murmurs. "Oh. That…that's my favorite bit too. But where, oh where did you learn to sing like that, so truly, so beautifully?"

The men shuffle about, looking at the floor.

"Well, Sir Mozart, we learned in school."

"In school?"

"Everybody in the country who goes to school learns music. We play instruments, too."

"You do? Which ones?"

"Oh, you know, oboe, flute, clarinet, bassoon, horn, harp. Sometimes off shift, we moonlight in dance bands and other places. We'd do it full time if we could, but there are too many musicians in Prague to make a decent living at it."

"The devil you say! Perhaps I can write you a cantata to celebrate Bohemia's Enlightened educational practice and the miracle of musical policemen. No, really, I mean it; I'll do it."

Mozart concludes that Praguers, even unto the minions of the law, truly *get* him, so much more so than the Viennese, the French, and the English all lumped together. He feels he could hardly be more loved and appreciated by all the denizens of this wonderful city and this lovely jail than he is in right now.

Hearing a commotion outside the door, and the familiar voice of their Chief, the policemen and turnkeys snap to attention. Mozart remains seated by the stove, dabbing at his eyes and studying the floorboards, thinking about texts for a cantata dedicated to the brotherhood of musicians who are also guardians of the peace.

"Stand up before your bitters!" bellows a familiar voice, reminiscent of the spawn of a ripsaw and a hunting hound. The composer raises his eyes to behold a lady standing before him, who, he vaguely recalls, is the Supreme Burgravess, Maria Elisabeth, Countess Nostic, the wife of his patron, Count Nostic, upon whose arm she is leaning heavily. Just behind them is a pale and cringing chief of police, who gestures mutely to Mozart that he should rise.

Mozart, both confused and annoyed, continues to sit.

"We have just heard," barks the noble lady, "that this Mozart person has gotten himself in trouble once again. It's not enough bad that he was expelled from the Three Lions for harboring a dead body in his rooms and indicting a riot, but now it seems he has killed Prague's excellent apotheosis in the Bertramka Villa!"

"Excuse me, I don't understand you, what are you saying? Sleeping, she was sleeping, not at all dead, and...."

"We hold this person responsible for bringing chaos and murder to our city, also for not completing the overture to our opera. Therefore, by officious decree of the Governing Body...."

"Now then, my dear," says the Count, gentling his gruff martial voice to a wheedling croon, "I get to say this bit, being the Head of the Governing Body; it's official business. If you would please allow me. By official decree of the Gubernium, Mozart is to remain incarcerated in this house, save during rehearsals at the National Theater, until the overture to *Don Giovanni* is finished, and until we have his sworn word that he will cause no more disruptions of the peace, do no more murders, and that the opera will be ready to perform on the fourteenth October, in time for...."

"Up shut, Nostic," bays his good wife. "I get to say *this* bit. This person will be ready to present his opera in time for the royal visit of the Archduckess Maria Theresa and her groombride, Prince Anton of Saxony. They are on their welding tour and will be attending the premiere of this play on the fourteenth of this month, and it had butter have an overshirt and be in perfect order throughout for their Highnesses, even if it means he has to spend all his hours in a sail jell!

"I, as president of the Noblewomen's Association, will not jeopardize the high importinance of this occasion by allowing any more crimes commissioned by that person. We have brought scored paper, quills, sand, and ink. We have arranged for Chief of Police Kretènček (who winces, shrugs, and stares at the ceiling) to stable him in a quiet cell, and for a guard of two ossifiers to export him to the theater for rehearsals and from it again when they are over. After the run of the show the Governing Body will indict and try him for the murder of Herr von Halsbrecher. We, as leaders of this city's nobility, demand these assurances from...."

"No."

"How dare he speak to me...."

"I won't do it. I'm not going to compose in a sail jell."

"Address this lady by her title, sir!...."

"Very well, most revered Count, I will begin again." Mozart rises from his chair and makes an exaggerated obeisance.

"Your Most Highty-Mighty Countess Nosepick, I am certain of three things: One: I, Mozart, who am on friendly terms with the Emperor, will not be addressed as 'he,' the way one addresses a servant. Two: I will not write any overture at all if I spend one more hour in this place. Three: given the inability of your Italian troupe either to learn, let alone master, their music, the opera cannot be ready for the consumption of anybody, common or royal, on the fourteenth. We will need at least two weeks more work, in my estimation."

"He will obey our witches, or...."

"Or what? If you throw me out of town, *meine sehr verehrte* Griffon, or issue threats to put me in the dock, you will get no overture, no show, and you might have a popular uprising of music lovers on your hands; how about that? Even the cops and jailers here are panting to see *Don Giovanni*. Who knows what riots and chaos might happen if it were cancelled?"

Mozart sees the Police Chief frantically gesturing for him to tone it down. He responds with the slightest of nods and calls upon his courtly manners.

"But let me make you a counterproposal, my dear Count and Countess, one that may suit you very well. We will put on *Le Nozze di Figaro* for the visitors instead. The troupe knows it by heart; and if they should all take ill and die, the rest of the city knows it by heart too and can probably stand in for them. You must admit that Figaro is the perfect play to play before newlyweds, since several of its personages become newly wed, right up onstage."

"Totally unsuitable," snorts the Countess.

"Really, dear lady? May I ask why?"

"They are all bastards! Figaro is a bastard. Rosina is a bastard. Susanna is a bustard. How can we present such illegible and low-class personages before a royal and noble young bridle? It is unthinkable. We must have *Don Giovanni*."

"But please consider, Countess! It's true that the Don Giovanni personage is of noble lineage, but he is, additionally, a rapist, a blasphemer, and a murderer. Donna Elvira, also a noble, has been messing around with said criminal without benefit of clergy. Zerlina, a peasant, is strongly considering adultery on her wedding day. Donna Anna, a noble, is telling fibs about how she spends her evenings. What sort of an example does that set for an innocent royal bride, I ask you?"

"I am certain, Mozart," says the Count, "that a few nights in the city lockup will make you see things differently. Come along, my dear. Give Chief Kretènček the writing supplies. We are late for lunch."

The noble couple execute a crisp about-face, arm-in arm. They sweep out, nearly crashing into Constable Pospíšil from Košíře, who has been home and back, as evidenced by his full uniform; he flattens himself against the wall, salutes and clicks his heels smartly. This reverence for Prague's most exalted beings accomplished, he enters the guardroom with an envelope of papers.

To Mozart he whispers, "Old Commander from my army days."

To his Chief: "Local surgeon's and investigative team's initial report, sir." He hands the envelope over.

"Should we escort Mr. Mozart to a holding cell while I read out this evidence?" muses Chief Kretènček

"No!" roars the crowd of turnkeys, policemen, *Putzfrauen* and casual passers-by who have drifted in to be in the presence of the famous genius who wrote *The Crazy Day*. "Let him stay here!"

The Chief shrugs and reads silently for several minutes. Finally, he fixes the composer with a hard stare. Mozart stares back in alarm as the Chief approaches him and examines his face at an uncomfortably close range. His lips. His cheeks. His eyebrows. His ears, his cravat. The Chief circumnavigates the composer, lightly brushing his hair and coat with his fingertips, which he then studies.

"Why," growls Mozart, "Are you sniffing around me like a brothel patron or a horse trader at the fair? Would you like to examine my teeth and hooves as well? Or are you leaning in for a kiss?"

Chief Kretènček flushes, shrugs and shakes his head slowly.

"It says here in this report, that the deceased…well, I must ask this, sir…are you ever inclined to wear lady's make-up?"

"Excuse me, but what the hell?"

"It says here that the late Herr Hambacher's face, mouth and neckwear were smeared with rouge and grease paint, and it goes on to say...."

"Since I was locked in alone with the good Apothecary all on a moonlit night, you assume we had arranged some kind of mad love-tryst that went bad, is that it? Well, how about the fact I was not always alone? Madame Dušek, who is guilty of having locked me up in there to begin with, came home from her concert engagement before dawn and, seeing her father dead on the floor, threw herself upon him and covered him with kisses and tears, consequently slathering him with her rouge, paint and mascara. I witnessed the whole terrible tragic scene. End of story."

"Well sir, not quite. The doctor also found white paint on the deceased's, ah, nether regions, and liprouge smeared all over his, his, his, you know. Did you happen to observe, at that time, Madame Dušek giving deceased a BJ?"

"Are you crazy? He was her *father* for God's sake! And dead! What would be the *point*? You can't accuse the bereaved! You might as well go back to accusing me of blowing Herr Hambacher, whom I have never even met. And! Your questions are totally ridiculous! You sir, are an idiot."

"Did you kill Herr Hambacher?"

"No. I have never killed anybody; but I have had, and am having, at this very moment, vivid fantasies about doing so."

"Very sorry sir, I was just doing my sworn duty. Personally, I wouldn't think you could do a murder, to look at you."

"Listen, idiot, being judged and found wanting as a murderer makes me even more eager to kill you. I forgive you because I know you can't help it, because you're an idiot. So, idiot, why don't you and I and the good soldier Constable Pisswhistle wander back out to Bertramka and gently interrogate the household concerning who else besides Madame Dušek might have access to her summer house? You might ask my dear wife if I was tricked out in paint like a Viennese whore or a Bohemian countess when she met me on the path from the summerhouse at the crack of dawn. And also, if you don't mind reading further in this report, could you tell me if Deceased had any, oh you know, wounds, perhaps?"

"It says here there were wounds."

"Aha! What kind of wounds? Fatal ones?"

"Bites. Shallow. On the neck."

"A vampire then!"

"It goes on to say, Candle wax on deceased and the floor. No blood, no vomit, no shit, a sizeable amount of piss, and pardon me, some jizz."

"I hereby confess to ownership of the piss. And the wax. When I stepped on the deceased I was scared pissless and dropped my candle. But I absolutely deny biting the man."

Say, Herr Mozart, you have a real nose for crime! I bet you could have solved those Vienna Burgtheater murders."

"Oh nonononoNO! There were *no murders* in the Burgtheater! And do not mention my nose either; it's a sore subject. Can't we please all return to Bertramka? I'm sure the investigating idiots missed some relevant clues, and I would like to go home to my wife and friends, and, for the love of God, get some sleep. Pretty please, Chief?"

"Oh, I don't know, sir, what about Count Nostic?"

"You think he did the murder? Shall we lock *him* up and make *him* write the overture to *Don Giovanni?*"

"Haha, you do like your little jokes, sir. The Count said by order of the Gubernium that *you* should be detained until *you* write it."

"Non più andrai…hm hm hmm…How would he know if we went back there? Unless our good constable Pisspot goes and snitches on us to his old Commander Nostic."

"I was infantry, not intelligence," mutters the Pospíšil.

"Oh, now," laments the Chief, "you've got me all confused. But orders is orders. Maybe you could write the overture while we go back to Bertramka and interview the household?"

"Oh, dammit, all right. If the Great Sebastian Bach could write the second twenty-four in prison, I can crank out a mere overture. Or maybe that small cantata I have in my head right now, instead. But! I am desperate for a nap. And lunch. Can I order in? Then I have to rehearse, at least a little, sometime today. When you go back out to Bertramka, don't forget to look into who else has the keys, all right? Favor to me?"

"Yes sir, thank you sir for the tips. You're pretty good."

"My wife is better. If you need any help detecting, just ask her."

Whenever I can find a moment, I daub on another little piece—but indeed I cannot stay at it very long, because I belong too much to other people—and too little—to myself...

Mozart to Gottfried von Jacquin, October, 1787

Constanze Visits her Husband in Jail

October 8, 1787

E tutto amore; chi a una sola è fedele, verso l'altre è crudele

In a raw and overcast late afternoon, Constanze arrives at the jail, having driven back to town with Chief Kretènček and his crime-scene squad. She brings snacks, beer, a change of linen and a little borrowed clavichord. Alas, she has discovered that the sketch of "Bella mia fiamma" and her husband's pipe and tobacco have been confiscated as evidence in the case. The officers greet the Great Man's wife with due deference, doing a casual search of her parcels—just checking for weapons, hacksaws and files, not that we are expecting to find any, dear Madame—and offering assurances that every possible comfort will be provided for the famous Mozart as long as he is their guest. She is led to the cozy guardroom and is soon joined by a very distracted Wolfgang.

Her husband, who has been in his cell sketching out "A Policemen's Cantata" on the manuscript paper that is supposed to have the overture to *Don Giovanni* written on it, sees his loyal little wife warming herself by the stove, and instantly assails her with a torrent of rage.

"Constanze, it's about damn time! Where have you *been*! You would not believe what has been going on in here! I was interrogated like a common criminal! The Nostics, our dear patrons, paid a call! I thought they would use their influence and fix it so I could be released on my own recognizance, but instead! The Count—no, the entire provincial government!—has condemned me to stay in this lockup until I produce an overture for *Don Giovanni*! Naturally, I refused to do so. What's more, Nostic's lovely Countess wife is threatening me with indictment and trial for murder if I can't get the show up by the fourteenth!"

"Why don't you just...."

"NO! I will not be bullied by him or her or anyone, and I will *not* be treated like a servant or a child! Who do they think they are, commanding such a thing? I don't write overtures under threat of punishment and that's that."

"But he's your patron, and you owe him an overture, don't you?"

"AND The idiot Police chief has surmised that I had somehow arranged a hot date at Bertramka with the late Herr Hambacher—may he be received extra-quick in Paradise—ignoring the fact that I never met the man in my life! He clings to the idea that I slathered makeup onto my face, gave Hambacher a blowjob and then murdered him."

"So I gathered."

"What does that mean, 'so you gathered?'"

"The police interviewed me at the villa. They wanted to know what you were wearing when I met you coming down the hill this morning. They asked us none-too-subtle questions about the state of your clothes, your secret kink for women's makeup, your amorous proclivities, and who has the keys to the summer house. So, I gathered."

"And what about the keys?".

There are four, and one is missing. Nonetheless, they are stubbornly, pruriently, fixated on the most unlikely tale of all: namely, your getting yourself up in greasepaint and making love to Herr Hambacher and cold-bloodedly killing him; then serenely composing an entire aria in a locked house, because who else could have done it? You have to admit it makes for a sensational story, no matter how unlikely it is."

"*Scheiss*! They're just deferring to Nostic, which I am never going to do even if I spend the rest of my life in jail! I won't abase myself to the Countess either. She wants *Giovanni* to play next week, and it's a shambles right now, and I told her it would be prudent to play *Figaro* instead. She refused to substitute Figaro, for her own personal reasons, barking insults at me as she went. I told her my show goes up when it's ready to go up, not when some princess or other waltzes into town."

"Did you really?"

"No. But the impulse was there."

"Who's running rehearsals in your absence?"

"Oh, I am. Morning rehearsal was cancelled. But after a nap and some lunch, they loaded me down with chains and two officers marched me over to the theater and stood guard over me all afternoon. Nostic's orders. They had such a wonderful time at rehearsal that the whole force is now lining up to pull Mozart-guarding duty, because it turns out they are all musicians on the side and are dying to hear the play. Dear good fellows, so appreciative. I'm writing them a cantata. What's happening at Bertramka?"

"Josepha collapsed as you know, then she took ill. She is running a fever and is confined to her bed. I look in on her and try to comfort Dušek and Clam. She seems to be in a deep fever-dream, so we have not spoken, nor did the police interview her today. They questioned the men though, who are also persons of interest because they both have keys to the summer house. They are free on their recognizance but are not permitted to leave Prague. I'll bring you some more of your things tomorrow if you are determined to remain here. I can see that nothing will change your mind, so enjoy your stay. Are there really chains?"

"No, but I wanted to inject some extra drama."

"Silly darling, there's already plenty of extra drama. I'll see you tomorrow evening. Love you so much, kisskiss!"

Constanze, after a tender leave-taking with her husband, scampers around the corner and into the town square for her hot date with Signor Bassi, who is waiting for her under the Astronomical Clock.

The Assignation

October 8, 1787

Là ci darem la mano

"Ah, my dear Madama Mozart, I, I...."

"You are so kind, Signor Bassi, I am delighted that you can take time out from your busy schedule. I really need some sort of diversion after yesterday's cannonade of calamities."

"But what has happened, Madama? And why is Signor Mozart escorted to the theater by the police?"

"Oh, there was a ruckus at the Dušeks, as you probably have heard; Madame Dušek's father died under strange circumstances after we left the Three Lions and moved out there. Count Nostic has ordered Wolfgang to be kept under guard at the jail until he writes the overture. But everything will be all right very soon. Let's take a stroll and do some sightseeing. Where shall we go?"

"The Horse Market."

"What's there?"

"Horses."

"Oh lovely! Wolfgang *loves* horses; he leases a nag in Vienna that he calls Rosinante, and rides him around the park. We love *dogs* too, we had a little dog, Gaukerl, that we boarded with friends when we visited here last winter, and the pup became so attached to their children we gave him up to them. Then we got another one, Kätherl; *she's* staying with my sister Sophie. And we love *birds* of course. But our most recent one, a singing Starling, died of old age. You remember that story about how the poor birdie and my father-in-law passed away in the *same week*...."

Constanze trips along arm in arm with her guide, babbling brightly about whatever pops into her head; keeping up a steady stream, because Bassi gazes mutely ahead and says nothing at all. He shyly grasps her hand and places his other hand on the small of her back to help her hop over a steaming pile of horse-shit. On the other side, he holds her other hand and looks directly into her face for a moment before ducking his head.

"Ah, Madama...."

"Ah, Madama what? Is there something you wish to say?"

"Ah, Madama...."

"All right then. I'm glad you got that off your chest. Anyhow, as I was saying, *Figaro* was so much better received here than in Vienna. Praguers *instantly* grasped the boldness and sophistication of the music. Did you know I got to sing Barbarina in the final dress rehearsal in Vienna? What a thrill to be in that show, just once, with all those splendid singers! have you heard Benucci? What an *artist*! And *so amusing* too! It was a *sensational* show, no matter how jaded the audience response was. Signor, are you feeling all right? You look rather pale."

"I don't know...."

"Well, let's go into this little tavern and rest a while. You must take some wine to fortify you. I hope you'll be well enough to rehearse tomorrow. Now sit down and let me feel your forehead. No fever at all. Can we have wine please? Ah, your pulse is beating rather fast; that's not so good."

Again Bassi takes the little hand whose fingers have lain so recently, so gently, on his wrist. With mournful, limpid, yearning eyes locking on her eyes, he says—nothing.

Constanze has become mesmerized, transfixed like a small animal before a cobra from India. For seconds, or perhaps minutes, possibly hours, the two gaze into each other's eyes. Neither moves a muscle, not even to breathe.

The wine arrives, and the spell breaks. They drink, sheepishly peering at each other over the edges of their cups.

"My dear young man, can you not tell me what ails you?"

"Madama, I don't know how. I am not so good with words. At the theater, or after rehearsals, the great Casanova tells us of his adventures traveling all over Europe, and he gives me a lot of advice. He told me always to remember this: 'The man who expresses his love to a woman in words is nothing better than a fool.' He has repeated this several times, so it must be true."

Constanze blinks and stares at Bassi.

"Casanova? And is he coaching you for your role in the play? Or are you testing the wisdom of his advice by trying it out on me?"

"I don't know."

"I am surprised to discover how well it seems to be working. Be frank with me now, and tell me— Are you or are you not, expressing your feelings to me in dumb-show at the suggestion of Casanova?"

"I don't know."

"It's unlikely that you would come up with a plan to make love to me all on your own. Not only am I married, but I'm ever so much older than you, too. I'm twenty-five, and have had two children. And you are only…?"

"Twenty-three."

"There, you see? Did Signor Casanova hint, imply, or advise you about why you should approach me?"

"He once said: 'An experienced girl can teach you a lot.'"

Constanze blinks again, furrows her brow, takes another sip of wine, and looks long again into the eyes of her tongue-tied tour guide.

"You know, Signor Bassi, I am really very fond of you. I like that you do not spew the usual shopworn *gallanteries* at me. I like that you find our situation confusing. Let's not say anything to each other for the rest of this evening. I'll just rest my hand on your arm, and we'll stroll around this lovely square, and every so often we'll stop and just look each other in the eyes. Would that be sweet for you?"

"I don't know. Yes."

Constanze reaches out and brushes his other hand lightly with her fingers. He enlaces his fingers with hers.

"You are a very, very sweet young man. Why don't we proceed?"

The Second Visit of Constanze to Mozart in Prison

October 9, 1787

Capisco, briconcella! Hai timor ch'io comprenda com'è tra voi passata la faccenda

"Darling, see what I have brought you! Fresh cravat, new handkerchiefs, hair ribbon, carpet slippers! Other odds and ends. Now your life as a prisoner is complete!"

"Wonderful woman that you are! Now I can compose in comfort. Except I miss my pipe and tobacco. It seems to be in the evidence lockup. I am almost done with a little piece I promised to write for the cops, and I can start on the orchestration of Josepha's aria."

"Are you going to write the overture?"

"No. Let the Nosepicks sweat."

"All righty then."

"So, what have you been doing with yourself while I slave behind bars and in the theater?"

"Let's see. Josepha stays in bed and does not speak. František and I have been reading through some of his songs. They are quite lovely, but in retrospect, one seems much like the other. But he plays so imaginatively I didn't notice until after. And yesterday I took a tour of the Old Square and the Horse Market."

"What's to see there?"

"An old clock. Horses."

"Did you wander around all by yourself then?"

"Well, Bassi asked if he could show me the sights, so I went with him."

"I know you did. One of the officers saw you."

"So what?"

"I don't like your being seen walking with him. It's an embarrassment."

"To whom? He offered; I thought it kind. It was a horse market. We looked at horses for heaven's sake! Are you really that mistrustful of my constancy?"

"Well...."

"Bassi is young and handsome; he's a star, and he's virginally shy and has no conversation. He gazes pathetically at me like a spaniel begging at the dinner table. I am rather flattered to be noticed, for once; but I don't plan to run off with him if that's what you're thinking."

"I am thinking that he believes he is Don Giovanni and he's trying out his moves on you. I don't like your spending even an hour with him."

"Well, sweetheart, he's a pretty poor excuse for a Don Giovanni in real life. Besides, he's working hard enough trying to be the dissolute Don at the theater. One hour's sightseeing stroll on his arm is not the violent rape of Zerlina, is it?"

"He should have been practicing his part in his free time. He makes too many mistakes."

"What do you suggest I do with my free time while you are at rehearsals, and locked up here every evening? Play endless duets with Christian or František at the villa?"

"Christian? So it's Christian now?"

"Or maybe should I knit? I have trunks full of baby clothes at home, and I'm sure Mama is making me some more. I need some exercise; I need to escape from that house of grief, and I get a bit of a kick strolling and sightseeing on the arm of my mute gallant, and even flirting with him a little. What harm?"

"Gallant?"

"Will you stop that, please? What's wrong with you?"

"Compared to that young gallant Adonis, your husband is a Mangelwurzel. The great genius has an ugly nose, a misshapen ear, a fat jiggly ass and scars all over his face. And whether Bassi is courting you in pantomime or declaiming passages from Shakespeare, he's making the Mangelwurzel jealous, that's what harm."

"Good. Everyone and their mother have always courted you, feted you, taken you out dancing and drinking and playing billiards, while I got to play the demure mouse of a wife sitting in the corner alone, if I am even invited along in the first place! I don't have much fun, except for that one time when I drank a bit too much and showed off my legs at Baroness Waldstätten's rowdy party, which you never ever have let me forget about!

"You think I was never jealous? I want some fun now; I'm bored to distraction; I'm not busy raising your child, I'm not running your household, mending your stockings, or walking your dog. And I like it when people pay attention to me!"

"And I don't pay attention to you?"

"Of *course* you do, but your attention is…doled out in installments, like the rent. Bassi's attention is being paid to me all at once, in a lump sum. He just blazes with attention, all the more because he is so silent. He looks in my eyes, he listens, and he shows me shy little courtesies. It's as if there is no one in the world but me; it's so intense! It's different with us married people…The humdrum of domestic life, and your work and my housekeeping; they dilute our passions a bit, don't they?"

Mozart's entrails contract like a fist. Where has he heard these words about lump sums before? Yes. Da Ponte. Quoting Casanova. Those oft-repeated infallible tips for the seduction of any woman. Give them everything that you are at that moment.

"Does Bassi…does he socialize with Casanova at all?"

"Casanova dines often with the troupe, probably prowling for sopranos. But yes, Casanova has been talking to him. Probably coaching him for his role as the Don, the old lecher, who better?"

"Constanze, I don't trust that man. He's evil. I heard that he bought little peasant girls in Russia and had his way with them! Remember how, only last year I believe, we were so shocked and appalled that a man would buy and violate a little girl?"

"I was not quite so shocked as you were, considering my sisters' various experiences with their patrons. Sweetie, look at your opera! Does not your Don Giovanni do the same, in Lorenzo's verse for 'Madamina.' '*Suo passion predominante, e la giovin principiante!*' His overruling passion is for little girls!" At least I think that's Lorenzo's verse…it could easily be Casanova's.…"

"Lorenzo likes grown-up women. Now you mention it, I don't think he would even write such a verse, after the revelations during *Figaro*. Maybe it really was the other one…Oh good God, let's just not conflate Lorenzo and Casanova and Bassi and Don Giovanni; it's too confusing and ugly!"

"You know, darling, Bassi plays mandolin. He's going to serenade me."

"Now *you* stop with the conflating! I know you're teasing me but I'm getting all sweaty and nervous. As for serenades…really? You mean—Did your little husband never, ever, serenade you?"

"No, and that's a fact."

"Have mercy. I wrote you fugues. I wrote you a trio. I wrote you an aria for the Vespers. I tried to get you into *Figaro*. Dammit, Constanze, serenade or no serenade, Bassi's not Don Giovanni and he's not…not…he's just a silly boy, and you- you're a matron several years older!"

"And Josepha is ages older than you, but you used to have a bit of a thing going with her, did you not?"

"Only two years older. Besides, she's a professional colleague."

"Ah. ha."

"Forget I said that. It was wrong, a mistake, a sin, I am slapping myself now, on the jiggly ass, on the tuberous nose…AND! I swear I will write you a serenade this very night! The most beautiful serenade ever heard in the civilized world and beyond, and you will hear it in less than a week!"

"I hate to bring this up, but you're in jail."

"Never mind. I can do it. I have hidden resources."

"All right. I'll forgive you if you serenade me under my window at Bertramka in the very near future. Swear!"

"I swear it, I swear it, I swear it on your lovely eyes. I swear it on our love!"

"See that it happens, Don Ottavio mine, or it'll be one whole year of no nookynook for you."

Da Ponte and Casanova Visit Mozart in Jail

October 9, evening

Cavalier voi siete già, dubitar non posse affè, me lo dice la bontà che volete aver per me

"What in God's name is that damned racket out front there?" Mozart stops playing and asks the singer nearest the door. The policeman, his freshly-written vocal part in hand, peeks out the door of the guardroom. He reports that two gentlemen have entered the Police Headquarters and are yelling at the duty officer in an incomprehensible language, possibly Italian mixed with German; and making threatening gestures.

"Oh no, no no no," murmurs Mozart. "Shut the door and lock it for the love of God!"

The shouting continues.

"*Wir müssen* Mozart seen, *du* hound *von* hell! Stand aside before I *snudo* my *spada! Weisst du nicht chi siamo? Ich bin* the Abate Da Ponte, *il poeta* of *Le Nozze di Figaro UND Don Giovanni,* and *dieser Mann* is *der uomo noto* Casanova, Ritter von Seingalt! We are here to pay a mercy visit to Mozart! So, *wo ist* the famous genius? In which dungeon does he languish?"

"Well, begging your pardon, most honored poet, and gentle knight," says the duty officer, "but he's in rehearsal in the guardroom at the moment, and can't be disturbed."

"He's rehearsing his opera in this jail?"

"No sir, but he has written a little choral cantata for the turnkeys and officers here, and they are doing a readthrough."

"Ah. Now that we have stopped shouting, I believe I do hear music…harp, clavier, winds…what the hell?"

"Why don't you make yourselves comfortable, honored sirs, until they are done? And permit me, Herr Da Ponte, to say how much we all enjoy your wonderful words to 'Non più andrai.' (sings a few bars, marches in place) You got it just right. You must have been a military man at one time, sir."

"No indeed, my good man. But a poet must be able to conjure in his imagination all sorts of things outside his sphere of experience. Or in my case, I just asked a soldier."

"Ah I hear voices, they're breaking up. Please come with me to the guardroom, sirs."

Mozart is noodling at his little clavichord and humming to himself as Da Ponte and Casanova burst into the guardroom.

"Amadeo, my poor prisoner! What the infernal fuck are you doing in here? I am shocked, appalled, distraught, unbelieving, and unnerved!"

"Mozart, you scalawag you! We meet again! How are you surviving incarceration?"

"So, Da Ponte," chirps Mozart, "you have arrived! How lovely! Come sit by me, dear friend, and tell me all the news from Court. And how was your journey? Do you have good lodgings? Have you tried the wild game with mushroom sauce at The Three Lions?"

"Staying with Casanova actually, at Waldstein's town house. Let's see.... Storace and her brother and O'Kelly left for England without her odious husband, and...Now you stop *distracting* me! You're in *jail*! Calaboosed! Detained! Enchained! Fettered! Gaoled! Hoosegowed! Immured! Jailed! Oops, repeating myself! But I could go on right through the alphabet!"

"Not necessary. I know where I am."

"Now that I think of it, our circumstances from last year have been reversed! Oh, the cruel irony of it! Never fear, I will do my best to get you out, which, upon reflection, is more than you did for me! Nevertheless, dear inconstant but nevertheless beloved friend, Da Ponte forgives all and flies to the rescue!"

"I am gratified, Abate."

"The Imperial quartermaster is coming in a few days from Vienna to arrange for the royal honeymoon festivities, and I'll speak to him about this monstrous outrage the moment he descends from his coach! He will put a stop to this terrible—"

"AND if all else fails," interrupts the roundly snubbed and deeply insulted

Casanova, "I'll show you how to escape from this sieve of a prison! It would take you two minutes and not two years, as in MY case, to wriggle out of here."

"Don't."

"How do you mean, 'don't?'"

"Don't pull strings with the quartermaster. Don't show me an escape route. Let me be, Signori. I like it here."

"*Scusi,* what?"

"They're such good company. The food is excellent. They sing divinely, they play instruments, they love me as a composer as I have never been loved before, except perhaps by my Papa. They get my music, as Papa always did, and they like to keep me close at hand, as Papa always did."

"You're joking!"

"I never joke. I've given it up. These simple policemen's affection makes me feel all warm inside. Besides I'm getting so much done. I'm orchestrating the concert aria I wrote for Madame Dušek, and then there's rehearsing the little cantata, and writing a piece for—never mind. I'm also tweaking some numbers in the opera to fit the singers better. I'm thinking about adding another solo *scena* for Donna Elvira, and I'm putting in finishing touches to the finale. Everything is going so well, except the overture of course, but that's another story."

"But—"

"AND, do you know, this lovely jail is the only place in town where I don't have to listen to 'Non più andrai' all day long. In the taverns, on the street, coming out people's windows. I'm surprised that damn mechanical clock hasn't been re-jiggered to play it on the hour."

"They sing it in here too. The on-duty just serenaded me with it."

"Well, I have forbidden them to do it in my presence, and they obey."

"What about your adorable wife?"

"She is sleeping a lot these days, and taking care of Madame Dušek, who is in mourning. Besides, she is angry with me."

"So, taking a little marital vacation?"

"Supplemented by a few strained visits."

"How can you possibly refuse a lovely woman's company," says Casanova, "while you are still young and possibly virile? I couldn't have done it myself.

But then, I have never married. Perhaps the thrill wears off and the act becomes routine.

"Speaking of thrills! Signor Mozart, allow me to present you with a complimentary copy of my pamphlet entitled *My Escape* as a token of our friendship. It explains how I escaped from the Palace of the Doges. Just in case you change your mind about staying here. It's hot off the presses and people are snapping it up."

Mozart breaks into song, "*Altre repliche non fo, no, no, no, no, no, non fo.*"

Da Ponte sniggers behind his hand and taps Casanova's shoulder.

"He's started singing, Giacomo; time to depart. Well then, my dear Masetto, Casanova and I will discreetly withdraw and not interfere with your peculiar life choices. Perhaps I will see you in the theater tomorrow morning."

"Yes, you would be a great help beating the words into the singers' thick heads, as I beat the notes. When they remember the words, they forget the music. When they remember the music, they forget the words. When they get onstage, they forget their own names AND the words AND the music.

"Are they that stupid?"

"These kids are not like our Viennese troupe. They don't learn their parts in a flash, leaving them plenty of extra time for intriguing, as the Imperial company does. What's more, they refuse to work on performance days. Frankly I want to shoot them all and invite random Pragers plucked off the streets to sing their parts instead."

"Signor Mozart," purrs Casanova, "lovely to see you, we're off for an evening of dissipation and debauchery! We leave you lolling in your love-dungeon. I was only going to stay a few days, but Lorenzo and I have both decided to prolong our visit, to watch the two of you hammer *Don Giovanni* into shape. Count Waldstein is off with his hounds, hunting something somewhere; and rattling around in his dank dark palace with nobody to talk to is my idea of hell, so we will meet again, no doubt"

"The Imperial Quartermaster will be overseeing the dressing of the Royal apartments and the theater house the day after tomorrow, but I won't mention your predicament to him, if you'd rather I didn't," says Da Ponte. "He could free you in the blink of an eye; he's the Emperor's voice you know. Always an option."

"You've started repeating yourself, which means it's time to part company. Good evening, I need to work. Thanks all the same, but I'm perfectly content where I am."

Only the young baritone—an astonishingly handsome but utterly stupid fellow—was unhappy that in the entire opera he had not been given one great aria worthy of his talents.

Alfred Meissner, *Rococo-Bilder*, 1871

A Contentious Rehearsal

The Theater, October 10, 1787

Non voglio più servir, no no no no no

The Adonis-like non-mangel-wurzelesque Luigi Bassi, who should be standing by backstage during Don Ottavio's aria—through which Signor Antonio Baglioni has been crooning with half the energy needed to sustain life—has instead been pacing nervously in the front of the audience house. At times, Bassi lurches toward Mozart, who is sitting at the clavier, playing and conducting and shouting encouragement to the tenor. Finally, Bassi plants himself facing the composer, once again performing his adorable pout. Mozart glances up at him while continuing to play.

"You're supposed to be standing by onstage, Bassi."

"I can't sing that aria."

"What aria do you mean?"

"The wine aria."

"What do you mean, you can't sing it? He stops playing and applauds his tenor; "Well-done, Antonio, take a break. Full voice next time, OK?" He stands up and glares silently at Bassi.

"What I mean is," continues the singer, "I *won't* sing it. I refuse to sing it. I don't like it. It doesn't suit me. It goes too fast. There's too many words. There's no place to breathe; I feel like I'm going die by the end."

"You *are* going to die by the end."

"That's not what I meant. That aria doesn't show off my voice. I need a big showpiece scene. I want you to write me something else."

"No."

"Why not? You re-wrote my duet with Zerlina, you change other singers' arias to suit them. So why won't you give me the big solo scena, with lots of *fioritura*, like the one Baglioni just sang? Why can't I have something like my aria in *Figaro*?

"Because, this wine aria, just as I have written it, is as close as Don Giovanni ever gets to revealing his truth. His truth is that he has no feelings. He has no secret heart. In the hollow place where his heart should be, there throbs only desire, an insatiable need for momentary pleasure, preferably at other people's expense. He tells his servant to get everybody drunk so he can rape the women unhindered and enter their names in his little ledger. That's his paramount joy in life."

"I don't care about all that."

"I know you don't, and that's why you don't get a *scena*."

"Count Almaviva was a bad man and *he* got a *scena*."

"True. But the Count has feelings, though, doesn't he? Think about it. He hates that a lowly person is marrying the girl he wants. He is afraid people will make fun of him for not getting that girl he wants. He aches to take revenge on Figaro, which he thinks will console him.

"These are not nice, sweet feelings, but they are feelings nonetheless. Besides, Almaviva kneels down and begs pardon at the end."

"But I'm the title character!"

"And you are also making love to my wife."

"I am not!"

"Did Casanova tell you to pursue my wife?"

"No! I swear! Well, yes, he did. He said I needed to practice being a libertine, and anyhow, if I flattered her with my attentions, she might make you write me a big *scena*."

"Well, I'm delighted that you have combined your rehearsing of libertinage with your pursuit of a big *scena*. Very single-minded of you. But your flirtation with my wife is officially over. At my request, she is giving you up. I suggest you find somebody else to practice on."

"Damn! How dare you…how dare you speak to me thus? You have insulted me very much, Signor! I challenge you, Signor!"

Everyone in the theater has stopped doing what they were doing for some time now and is hanging on every word—now operatically loud—that Mozart and Bassi are saying.

"Get your sorry ass onstage, you ignorant muttonhead," shouts the composer, "and stop making a fool of yourself, or I'll have you and Panziani switch roles, and you can sing Leporello instead, how would you like that?"

"No! I won't do it! I'll fight you to the death! I demand satisfaction! Draw your sword, sir!"

"I see you have already drawn your sword, but it's made of wood, and you got it off the prop table, didn't you, you blinking idiot? I have a real sword, but it's a child-size one, and it's back in Salzburg, I think. So, not swords."

"Pistols then!"

"All right, pistols. Just pop around to the jail after dinner, and we'll take turns firing at each other in the guardroom. But I feel bound to warn you that I happen to be a celebrated marksman."

"*You?* No! Really?"

"I, yes, really. I, my sister, and our late parents, may they be reunited in Heaven, were all dead shots in the old Salzburg days. We got Tyrolean air rifles and held target shooting contests with them. We used to draw caricatures of all the people we hated on little cards and set them up as targets in our back garden. Cash prizes were offered to the one who shot our various enemies' portraits right between the eyes. I won quite a lot, and since you are my enemy right now, I don't see how I could lose."

"I-I- can't shoot at all."

"How about billiards then? We'll play a few rounds, drink a few rounds, and the winner gets my wife. But no *scena* for you. What do you say to that, pretty boy?"

"Billiards, all right then."

"Good. Don't you ever defy me ever again, or I will shoot you. And don't ride your voice so hard. If you go on forcing it like that you'll end up with a very short career. Fix it! And now *sul palco, raggazzino,* get up onstage little boy, and sing the wine aria, and I don't care if you turn blue and drop dead."

The Serenade

October 10, evening, Bertramka

Deh vieni alla finestra

Constanze and Josepha are wrapped in shawls, curled up on the music room divan sipping coffee, comforted by the warmth of the little porcelain stove. They are silent. This is the first time Josepha has left her bedchamber, where she has lain delirious, suffering from alternating chills and fevers. The older woman's head droops and her eyes are shut. She has sought out her friend this evening in her first effort to take up some sort of life again, or at least, perhaps, to talk about it.

"Please, my dear, forgive me for being such a dull conversationalist. I have no energy right now, but I find I need a woman's company. František is a rock, and Christian keeps telling me to cheer up. But you, who have lost a beloved father, and a father-in-law as well…you understand what severing that bond is like. Let's not speak of it just now; why don't you tell me what you have been doing these past few days?

"I'm so glad you are over your illness. You don't have to say a thing if you don't wish to. I'll just prattle on and save you the trouble. Wolfgang tells me there are bitter arguments and complaints at the theater, and he has put down some rebellions in the cast. My poor dear man is getting a lot of composing done in jail; tweaking the airs, polishing the finales, and writing some sort of occasional piece for the policemen, imagine that! And he is orchestrating your new air, of course. He works on everything but the overture.

"As for me, things are quieting down. I've stopped promenading with my handsome admirer; my feet swell up from too much walking now. Besides, some cop snitched on me to Wolfgang, and we fought about it. Besides again, something all too romantic was developing with Luigi."

"Go on, I am all ears."

"I'm surprised at how tongue-tied he is. He doesn't compliment or flatter or cajole or recite poetry. He just looks, with those big, sad, dewy, hungry eyes of his, straight into my own eyes. He's something of a simpleton, but…you know, it's very compelling, this mute looking. I began to have feelings: some wordless, deep connection to him somehow. I had to stop, because…I was getting, you know, aroused. And Wolfgang could see what was happening; he's no dummy. We were both annoyed with each other."

"I'm sorry. I understand you completely. In the dark of my grief for Papa, I saw how shallow and mean my charade with Casanova was. My actions were not becoming of a woman who is as deeply cherished as I have been and continue to be. I suppose was trying to prove some point or other, but I don't remember what it was now."

"Something about free-thinking, and women having erotic desires equal to men."

"Perhaps more than men, I believe, and different as well. We have deeper desires than the wish for unbridled debauchery. Casanova, like our Don Juan Tenorio, has no guilt, no shame, no remorse, and no ethics that I can discern. He is emblematic of the darker side of the Enlightenment and free-thinking, that is: not to be bound by any rules at all except those of self-interest. I don't wish to claim equality with men on that score."

"I still wish Wolfgang were not quite so jealous about my innocent flirtation with Bassi."

"But it was not quite innocent, was it?"

"No, you're right, but…."

"And how jealous were you of me because I flirted with Wolfgang ten years ago?"

"Plenty. I almost declined meeting you for lunch. But with Luigi…. I think I had a point to prove too—to myself, and to Wolfgang: that I am not just Mrs. Genius, that I have a heart and a will and needs of my own, and I loved that other men might think I'm worth courting for my own sake. But Luigi didn't give a fig for me or my charms; he wouldn't have looked twice at me until he was put up to it by that nasty old Venetian. I'm still pissed-off at all three of them!"

"But the memory of Bassi is rather sweet, yes?"

"Exceedingly sweet. *Basta*! Have we heard any word from the Coroner's Office? A self-serving question, I know, but I wouldn't mind having my jealous husband back; I don't care if we throw crockery and scream at each other like cats, as long as we come to terms afterwards. *Ma poi fa pace.*"

"Of course you will make peace. You care for each other despite all the storm and stress. As to the Coroner's report, there is still no word, only the doctor's initial findings, which were horrible enough to consider. A possible murderess-lover, *Ach Gott*!"

"Chief Kretenček tells me that the Coroner's Office is notoriously slow to produce documents. Wolfgang and I would like to know how, and who, and why...."

"Oh, My poor dear Papa...."

"There, there, my darling, weep as you need to. It's out of our hands. All we can do is wait, grieve, and love whom we love."

"*Entschuldigung*, Madame, I'm sorry to interrupt," says the maidservant who has entered the music room, startling the two embracing women. "But Andrej tells me that there is a large group of police officers assembling on the front lawn!"

"Oh heaven preserve us, what do they want now? Have they not interrogated, inspected, and arrested quite enough?"

"Maybe they want to interview you," says Constanze. "But why send so many officers then, when just one would do? And why at this late hour?"

"They told Andrej to request both ladies' presence on the balcony," says the maid, "'for a short colloquy that will be of deepest interest to them.' And Madame, they are in dress uniforms."

"With sashes?"

"And plumes."

"In that case, we had better go and see them, hadn't we, Constanze?"

The two friends take up their shawls and walk hand-in-hand to the center of the house and open the French doors onto the little balcony. They peer down at a small band of men standing in a pool of golden light. Some are holding musical instruments, some holding small pieces of paper, others lifting lanterns on poles. At the sight of the women, six men lift flutes, clarinets, bassoons, and horns and begin to play a music of heart-stopping beauty and tenderness. After a time, two men begin to sing:

Secondate auretti amiche
Secondate I miei desiri
E portate i miei sospiri
Alla dea di questo cor.

Voi che udiste mille volte
Il tenor delle mie pene;
Repetete al caro bene
Tutto che udiste allor.

Help me, friendly breezes
Help my desires
And carry my sighs
To the goddess of my heart.

You who have heard a thousand times
The tenor of my woe
Repeat to my dear one
All that you heard then.

At the final cadence the lanterns are extinguished, and   the platoon of
musicians steals away beneath the trees. The unearthly sweetness of the music
lingers like a fragrance in the starlight. The two women, having stood rapt and
quietly weeping throughout the serenade and for many minutes afterward, fall
into each other's embrace, and no words are spoken. Finally, Josepha whispers,

"That was the most sublime thing I have ever heard or will ever hear. Did
you know he was writing this?"

"No, I mean yes, but I forgot about it until now. I am just—melted to a
puddle! I forgive him everything, my poor dear darling!"

"I hope he keeps the manuscript safe. He needs to use that music in
whatever his next opera will be. I feel as if I have been lifted up into heaven
from the depth of grief!"

"Everything begins afresh. We are re-born."

"All our old intrigues look silly now, do they not?"

"Yes, yes, I think so. But I have an idea. I'll visit the Police House tomorrow, naturally. But please, allow me to do some modest investigations into your Papa's tragic death, in behalf of us all. I need to find out things that will liberate my husband; I am going to interview Chief Kretenček and make some delicate inquiries among my female acquaintances in the opera troupe."

Constanze Makes Another Visit to the Jail

Prague Police Headquarters, 9:00 A.M. October 11, 1787

Sarete sempre mio? Sempre!

Constanze arrives at the Police House promptly the next morning. She is escorted to the guardroom, where her husband is already at work. After she enters, the good duty officer discreetly shuts and locks the door but stays within hearing distance—as, he now suddenly recalls—he has been trained to do. What he hears are sobs, broken words, tender murmurs, and—he allows himself to imagine—sweet kisses, and so on and so forth. He looks at the floor and hums a tune to himself. It is last evening's serenade.

When the guard detail arrives to walk the famous genius to the theater, Constanze, her hair and fichu re-arranged and her skirts smoothed, declines their invitation to join them, saying she has some other business to attend to, if they would tell her where she might find Chief Kretenček. In his private cabinet with a new officer, was the reply.

"What are you up to, wench?" whispers Wolfgang.

"Sleuthing, Pooki, nothing more," she whispers back.

* * *

Constanze finds Chief Kretènček and another officer in the Chief's office, in deep conversation. She knocks quietly on the doorframe.

"*Guten Morgen*, dear Madame, I fear you are a bit too late for a visit with your husband. Have you brought him some more goodies?" says the Chief, as both policemen bow low to her.

"I have already seen him this morning; but now I would like a brief word with you, dear Chief. And this officer…is he not the Constable of Košíře? I believe we met briefly, on the day of the tragedy at Bertramka."

"Pospíšil, seconded to Prague to aid on this case, Frau Mozart!"

Both men speak at once, the Chief's baritone mingling with Pospíšil's tenor. Constanze starts, bursts into tears, and points at them with both fluttering hands.

"It was *you*, wasn't it? Last night, under the balcony...the duet...you sang...I hear your voices speaking together now and I am almost certain of it!"

Both men blush and rub their chins. "We admit it, Madame, it was us singing. I hope you were as pleased to hear that music as we were to perform it," murmurs Pospíšil.

"Pleased? I was transported! Never was there such a gift, in all the world! I am *so* grateful to you and to all the other musicians too!" Constanze embraces them both, steps back and gazes at them with moistly shining eyes. They gaze moistly back, bowing low once again, their hands on their hearts.

"Now, even though I am eternally in your debt, I would like to ask a small indulgence. Might my poor dear husband have his pipe and tobacco back?"

"I don't know, Madame. It was confiscated as evidence."

"Yes, but...he always writes overtures while smoking it. It helps him concentrate. For ensembles, he needs beer. Do you think we could lend him the pipe so he can carry out Count Nostic's command?"

"Madame, I am not sure we can bend the rules, even to get the overture onto paper. That pipe might be important evidence."

"You know best, of course. But is a little pipe as important as finding out who had access to the summer house? Did you ask who had keys?"

"Pardon me, Gracious gracious lady; do you think we neglected to ask the household about the keys? There are four keys altogether, Herr Dušek's and Count Clam's, which they showed to us willingly. Then there are Herr Hambacher's and Madame Dušek's. The crime scene team found one key seated in the summer house lock when they arrived. That one is in the evidence lockup. Since we have been unable to interview Madame, we don't know if that key is hers or her late father's."

"Was it on the outside?"

"Outside, Frau Mozart."

"Probably Madame's key then, don't you think? She could have left it in the lock at dawn, after she unlocked the door and found Mozart with the...her father."

"Mozart corroborates," says Pospíšil. "'She used her key to unlock the summerhouse,' he said to me. Since he was howling bloody murder (I beg your pardon dear lady, wrong word!), she probably forgot to withdraw it."

"Anyone," says Kretènček, "in possession of a key is automatically person of interest. Except the Deceased, of course."

"Even Madame? Do you suspect her?"

"We are watching all their movements. And we will interview Madame when she is well enough. All three of them had access and were on the premises that evening."

"Did you search my husband for the fourth key?"

"Standard procedure. It wasn't on his person. He could have tossed it, though."

"He could have let himself out with it too, but he didn't. Did you look for it in the vineyard?"

"True enough. Yes, we did some combing. No results."

"Are you watching anyone who didn't have access?"

"Casanova. We don't trust that fellow."

"Nor do I. How is he involved in this case?"

"Cheats at cards. Has a record. He's been thrown out of more cities than I've ever been in. He's trouble. A womanizer."

"You don't suppose Herr Hambacher was entertaining someone in the summerhouse, do you?"

"As a matter of fact, that is our theory; a woman, based on the evidence all the rouge and greasepaint smeared on the body."

"I'd guess, if she were a low type of woman, that she took Herr Hambacher's key after he was dead, locked the place up again, and ran away. Was he known to hire women for sex?"

"Well, we don't think the suspect was a common prostitute. The makeup she was wearing was top of the line. We are assuming the person was a lady of some rank."

"Or an actress, perhaps?"

"By God, we didn't remember about the theater people. But they do go for the best face paint, now I think of it," says Kretènček. "Very clever of you to notice, Frau Mozart.”

“Not likely an actress,” says Pospíšil, “A man wouldn’t bring such a woman to a respectable suburban district like Košiře and sneak her into a grand lady’s villa, would he? More like up against a wall in an alley, I’d guess.”

“Mind your tongue, Pospíšil,” snaps Kretènček.

“Sorry.”

Constanze blushes, smooths her skirts again, and dabs at her face with her hankie. She composes herself and continues on a different track.

“Do the police know when Madame and Herr Dušek returned from their concert tour?”

“No, why?”

“Well, she wrote me a note on the fourth, saying she was just back from Poland, and would I have lunch with her on the fifth; so maybe her father felt free to use the summer house on the third, say, for a bit of dalliance. He could have been killed on the third or the fourth as well as the fifth, which is when we arrived. Was there rigor?”

“No, but it’s not known if rigor had passed, or had not arrived yet.”

“What was he like in life, anyway? I don’t know anything about him.”

“A very respectable and well-to-do man, he was. A widower for some years now, seemingly content with his single state; never seen at the brothels. He was a commoner, but mingled easily with people of rank, him being of some use to them when they were ill and so on. People say he had a good sum of money invested in Countess Nostic’s family business in Germany; he had some sort of sweetheart deal with her.”

“What business is that?”

“Minerals and mining. Iron, lead, salt, such like.”

“Oh. Not very pertinent to this case, is it? Did he have any rivals or enemies?”

“Nobody makes an enemy of an apothecary; he could slip poison into their medicine, and who would know, eh?”

“But what about the mysterious woman poisoning the apothecary? Or wounding him somewhere nobody has noticed?”

“Pretty far-fetched, a poisoning, don’t you think? The only wounds discovered so far are from teeth. We wait upon the Coroner’s report.”

"Poisoning is not half as far-fetched as the Famous Mozart or the suspicious woman gnawing him to death. But consider: you have many pages of music sketches in your possession to prove he was extremely busy composing an aria on the night in question, and he wasn't on the premises the previous nights."

"But still the Ministry of Justice has been encouraged to think that the prime suspect is Mozart. He, being locked in with him, must have killed him; who else could it be? They are preparing an indictment, in the teeth of the evidence, so to speak, ha ha."

"But! *But*! Wolfgang had no motive, no means, no acquaintance, and no time. Please, dear officers, I want him back. Could I not bail him out? He is hardly a flight risk; he's in the middle of a production."

"Nostic forbids it. Because of the other thing, you know. He's a magistrate as well as the owner of the theater. Without his say-so there wouldn't even be a production, overture or no overture."

"But! This mysterious woman is obviously the culprit! I see that now! Listen! Whore or lady, whoever she is, after her murderous act, she would have coolly rifled her victim's pockets and found the key! Or, perhaps it had been left in the lock on the inside to ensure their privacy! Either way, she locked the door behind her, proving she was a callous and calculating person. She may have stuffed the key into her pocket bag and run off until she got to the river, tossed it in, and made her way to her home. That key may never be found, even if you drag the river!"

"Now calm down, dear Frau Mozart," says Kretènček, "all of those actions could have been taken by Madame Dušek herself, couldn't they? Perhaps father and daughter fought about something on the fourth and came to blows in a struggle, and her *Geschmink* got all over his person; or perhaps she poisoned him with something from his own shop; who knows?"

"But then why would she then invite us to Bertramka, after having killed her beloved father in the summer house, and why in hell would she proceed to lock Wolfgang in with him?"

"Well, to cast suspicion on him and divert it from herself."

"Josepha would *never*! She and my husband are old friends and professional colleagues, and she reveres his music! How could you even think she would betray him like that when he was writing her a new aria?"

"Just following the clues, Frau Mozart," says Kretènček.

"And ignoring the blowjob!" shouts Constanze.

"Pardon me," says Kretènček gently, "but it's easy to see why you are interfering with our investigation here. You are trying to make a good case for its not being your friend nor your husband neither. We'd love to set him free, but we are bound to go strictly by the book. Besides, everyone would suspect that you had a strong personal bias in his favor and came here to influence us."

"I do have a bias. I miss him terribly. But you're right; it would go against Nostic and the courts if you let him out because I begged you. Better he stays here and out of trouble. How is he behaving, by the way? No practical jokes, I hope?"

"Good as gold, from the first," says Pospíšil. "He was none too pleased about being locked up twice in the same day, poor man; but he did not resist arrest and came along like a lamb, and a lamb he has been ever since."

"Well, I'm glad he behaves nicely for you. One never knows."

Some of the leading ladies here (especially a particularly illustrious one) were pleased to find it very ridiculous, improper, and whatever else, that Figaro...should be given for the princess. In short, the ringleader through her eloquence took things so far that the impresario was forbidden by the Government to produce this opera on that day. And so she triumphed! "Ho vinta" she called out...from her box; — She certainly never suspected that the "ho" might be changed to a "sono."

W.A. Mozart to his friend Gottfried von Jaquin, 1787

Le Noble Trumps the Countess Oberstburggräffin Nostic

The Nostic National Theater, October 12, 1787

Lasciala, indegno, battiti meco!

The Towering Genius composer of *Don Giovanni* arrives with his police guard for his ten o'clock onstage rehearsal. On the stroll over, he asks the two officers if he might, in future, make the journey to and from prison unattended, on the honor system. He is met with indignant protests. Not possible! Not only do all the officers draw straws every day to pull Mozart duty, because they love attending rehearsals of this astounding new opera before anybody else in town hears it; but what's more, too bad, it's what their dear good Supreme Castle Count Nostic has ordered them to do, and they won't hear another word about it.

Mozart, touched by the affection of his jailors, and in a happy mood for once, enters the theater to find it overrun with people: the stage crew are swarming everywhere, fixing swags and festoons of evergreens and plaster fruit, wheat sheaves, ribbons, and medallions onto all the boxes, the proscenium, and the railings of the orchestra space. The chandeliers, groaning with banners, are being drawn back up. Nails are being hammered, ladders erected. Shouts and whistles drown out singers' warm-up vocalises.

"What's all this business? I need to rehearse my cast, which means absolute dead silence in the house! Who the hell is in charge here?"

"I am," says an elegant man holding a roll of wired ribbon and a sheaf of notes.

"Good God, I beg your pardon; it's Count von Eldersberg from Court! Da Ponte told me you were coming and what with my being in ja—in rehearsal and everything, I forgot about it! How do you do, *verehrte Graf* Imperial Quartermaster?"

"Very well, dear Herr von Mozart. We meet again, in happy circumstances. I'm overseeing the festivities for the visit of the Emperor's niece and her new husband, as you see. Yesterday I saw to the royal apartments in the Castle, in sad disarray if I may say so, after our late Empress spent so much money restoring them. Also I organized the menus and the extra servants. I must say the food here is excellent, better even than in Vienna. Today we dress the theater for your grand premiere, which I am extremely eager to witness. I see you have a police detail guarding you."

"Yes…the fans, you know; it's crazy here. They mob me in the street and try to snip of bits of my hair and clothes. Hence, you see, my need for personal bodyguards."

"And you, dear Count, you have been so busy! So thorough, so organized, as always! So preoccupied, indeed, that somebody forgot to tell you we are presenting *Le Nozze di Figaro* instead of the Don Juan opera, because of production delays and some, ah, last-minute musical adjustments I am making. In any case, *Figaro* is ever so much better suited for a wedding party, given the subject matter—the double wedding etc.—don't you agree? And the cast, nay, practically the whole town, knows it by heart. One musical brush-up tomorrow and a staging mark-through the day of, and we will be ready."

"*Figaro* will *not* be played! Over my dead body will *Figaro* be splayed before the Dutch-Archessness, niece of the Emperor! I have spooken!"

Le Noble startles and looks wildly around. Everyone pauses and turns to look up at up the Estates box at the front left mezzanine of the audience house.

"Where is that horrible and incomprehensible shrieking coming from?" whispers Le Noble. "Is the shrieker addressing you or me?"

"I am in charge here! *I own this theater*! I oversee this theater and all that happens in it! Just let that squeaking pin-feathered squab of a Mozart have a look at this officious decree!"

Count Le Noble von Eldersburg has located the origin of the shrieks: it is Countesss Nostic, swaying unsteadily at the front of the Estates box, holding tight to the railing as she tosses a piece of paper down onto Mozart's clavier.

"Just read that! *Ho Vinto*! I've beaten you, Mustard!"

"I am so deeply flattered, your Sublime Burgcountessness, that you now address me directly, and more or less by my name! Our friendship blooms apace!" responds the composer, grinning like a jack-o'-lantern while not making the required obeisance.

A stagehand picks up the paper and walks it over to the Imperial Quartermaster, who reads it and addresses the composer sotto voce.

"Hmmm. Mozart, can you tell me who is this gabbling harridan, and why does she toss official government papers around the theater, and why is she trying to ban *Figaro* from the stage and replace it with *Don Giovanni* if it's not ready to play? And why is the Governing Body making an official decree about it?"

"She is the head lady of Prague, and the wife of the Supreme Count of the Castle and head of the Gubernium, and distinguished military hero Count Nostic, who is also the founder and owner of this theater. As you can tell, we are being addressed by a woman of great influence. And charm. She, although not her noble husband, has a notion that every character in *Figaro* is a bastard, except Count Almaviva, who just behaves like one. Being of exalted birth and rank, the Countess finds *Figaro* just too scandalous. I have gently explained to her that *Don Giovanni* is way more scandalous, besides not being quite ready for public consumption yet. But she won't budge."

"Oh dear. These provincials! Well, Mozart, I am going back to the Castle soon, and I will, in the name of our Emperor, override this ridiculous decree. Right after lunch. Have you had the pheasant confit they make here? Heaven.

"But as I was saying, I am empowered to speak for our Emperor concerning anything in and around these royal festivities; and since the word of our great Kaiser is even more powerful than this squawking Countess's, you may 'count' on *Figaro*'s playing, as it were; you see, I made little joke there."

"Hahaha. Thank you, dear Count, for intervening, and ensuring that *Don Giovanni* will not be from the womb untimely ripp'd in Prague. And now let us part, because we both have work to do, and meals to eat."

Mozart sweeps an extra-low bow to the Count, who gives his notebook and ribbon to an assistant, and leaves the house with pheasant on his mind.

Putting away his courtly manners, Mozart stalks in the direction of his clavier, which is situated below the Estates Box. He seats himself, with his impertinent back to the noblewoman, who leans over the railing.

"*Ho vinto!*" roars the Countess again. Mozart leaps up and turns to her with blood in his eye.

"You'll soon change your tune to '*sono vinta,*' Contessa Nosepick!!" he shrieks, pointing an impolitic finger at her.

"I'll have my revenge on you," he continues, "for interfering in matters about which you know nothing!"

"Over my bed doddy you will! *Over my dead body!*"

"*Così sìa,* your high-and-mightiness! *So sei es*! Let it be so! Mustard has spoken!"

He turns his back again on the Countess again and stalks off, rage and defiance shaking his small person. He sees all the stagehands, singers, costumières, perruquiers, and carpenters gawking at him, and he glares back at them. At the same time, he is thinking that perhaps he has gone a bit too far.

* * *

And it comes to pass that a new edict from the Gubernium, commanded by the Emperor himself, is handed down on 12 October, stating that *Le Nozze di Figaro,* the Italian opera—not the scandalous, salacious and seditious stage play of the same name—may be performed in the city.

After a Sitzprobe and a quick brush-up rehearsal onstage, that opera is presented in the Nostic National Theater before the royal couple, with all the high-ranking personages of the town attending (assiduously guarded, or perhaps not, by a special detail of happy policemen), on 14 October, with the theater fully illuminated and decorated, and with Bondini's little troupe singing and acting to perfection.

After Act I ends with the megahit tune "Non più andrai," followed by a long, standing, stamping howling ovation, there comes a reading of an even longer celebratory poem dedicated to the Prince and his lovely bride. The pair endures this punishment standing at attention at the front of the Estates Box, and looking sovereignly bored.

When the poem is finished, the newlywed royals abruptly and conspicuously sweep out and do not return. They do so without any word of acknowledgment to their hostess of the evening, the *Oberstgraffürstin* Countess Nostic. An hour after midnight, when the crew arrives to strike the decorations and set up the stage for the next day's rehearsals, the janitor finds that noble lady's dead body sprawled on her divan in the Estates Box private lounge, with a bullet hole between her eyes.

Mozart Resists Arrest

October 15, 1787

E un orribile tempesta minacciando, o Dio, mi va!

Count Nostic arrives a little later, along with the police. He accompanies the body of his wife to the Coroner's Office. The police do a thorough search of the theater but find nothing but a bullet hole in the thin wall separating the front of the box from the private chamber behind it. A hard grilling of the night watchman follows. The poor man claims he neither saw nor heard anything, no gunshots, no sounds of an intruder, or any argument or struggle. He remembers that the Count and Countess sometimes dined late and even spent the night in their private chamber after the spectacle was finished and the building was locked up for the night. He is accused of drunkenness and dereliction and dismissed on the spot.

When Mozart and his escort of the day arrive at the theater shortly before ten, he encounters Chief Kretènček in the audience house.

"Dear Chief, *Grüss Gott*! What brings you here? Are you joining the opera-loving and Mozart-guarding detail today? Is it because I asked to walk over here on my own yesterday, and you suspect I might make a run for it?"

"Excuse me sir, but there was a murder committed here last night."

"Oh, Sweet Jesus with a Toothache, don't *say* that to me! I don't do murders in theaters! You're joking, right? Ha Ha! Ha? Now look, I'm busy here, trying to keep *Don Giovanni* from dying on the vine, or the wine, and you prank me with wild tales of murder! No! Nonono!"

"It was the Countess Nostic, sir. Somebody shot her last night as she slept in the Estates box."

"Are you serious? Why only yesterday I was conversing with her on this very spot, talking about the merits of *Figaro* versus *Don Giovanni*, rather warmly as I recall...."

"You were heard threatening her, sir, emphatically threatening. And pointing."

"No I didn't! Oh shit, yes I *did*! Well, I was a bit angry and may have said some intemperate things. But surely...."

"How angry were you, sir? Would you like to come the Police House and make a statement?"

"Are you arresting me? I won't go, and that's final."

"Are you resisting arrest sir?"

"You can't arrest me."

"Why not?"

"Because, idiot, I already live in your jail, and what's more, I was there all last night, locked up by my escorts. Yoo-hoo, there, Honor Guard! Where was I last evening? Tell him."

"Locked up tight in your cell after rehearsal, sir. That's right. We marched him back to the jailhouse and shut the door on him. Unless he's a sorcerer or an escape artist, he stayed there all night until we brought him here this morning."

"I am so grateful for your company, suddenly! Thank you a thousand times for keeping a sharp eye on my whereabouts."

"Mr. Mozart sir," says the Chief, "we discovered a pamphlet on 'how to break out of prisons' in your cell this morning."

"I haven't read it. Casanova gave it to me last week, but I wasn't interested in his escapades. I enjoy my incarceration. It keeps me out of trouble. Or so I used to think.

"And now I see my cast wandering onto the stage for the first act finale, so I am now through with you, Chief Kretènček. Be assured that I will return like a good boy, and we will rehearse the cantata as usual after dinner in the guardroom. Now get out of my way, I have things to do."

"All right sir, but let me give you a piece of advice: you are a person of interest in two murder cases, so you had better not go around threatening people and pointing your finger, or harboring escape manuals. Or practicing sorcery. Many eyes are watching you."

"Thanks, good morning, see you tonight."

Constanze and the Saporitis Go for Drinks

October 18, 1787

Finch'han dal vino

"Well, this is a festive occasion!" says Caterina Bondini, née Saporiti. Her sister Teresa Saporiti chimes in, "We haven't gotten together since *Figaro* and the Lenten balls! Wild times, right?" They both laugh their tinkling singer laughs.

"So lovely to see you both," says Constanze. Let's order some wine and some little dishes and have a good gossip! My treat!"

"A dish-and-bitch session, is what we'd call it!" laughs Caterina.

"A toast! A toast to Don Giovanni, the dissolute man punished! May all villains be punished and may the innocent go free!"

"Drink up and please have some more! I'll have just a sip, I have a little upset tummy; the child, you know."

"Dear, darling Connie, congratulations! Now tell us all the news from Court! How are your very famous sisters doing in the Palace Theater?"

"Oh, have you met my sisters too?"

"We know *of* them certainly. We have heard Aloyisia sing, in Dresden perhaps? She is quite good we think," Teresa Saporiti says, "even if she does lay on the grand diva act a little too thick, or so we hear; that sort of bitching only annoys the management. How is dear Madame Lange getting by after having been kicked out of the Burgtheater?"

"Oh, that's such moldy old news. Do the Vienna papers arrive *that* late here? Aloysia is doing extremely well. The management begged her to come back, soon after that incident, because she's indispensable. Now she is singing a run of *The Abduction*, in that very Burgtheater, and working in Schikaneder's theater on alternate days. And, Madame Saporiti, are you spending your free hours with Abate Da Ponte? I hear he's decided to postpone his departure to help put a finish on the show. I know you are such great good friends. Can we have more wine please?"

"Such a lovely man, such a witty poet! I suppose you mean that he stuck my name into the *Giovanni* finale as a personal tribute to me. '*Ah, che piato saporito,*' hahaha! I must catch up with him before he goes back to his duties at Court. He too is indispensable everywhere! We are certainly good and great friends, but dear Lorenzo is a friend to all women, if you get what I mean, and I'm sure you do. Speaking of free hours, how are you enjoying being courted by Casanova's debauchery student, our young Signor Bassi?"

"Ah, dear, sweet, Luigi. I miss his company terribly. The boy was so kind to offer to show me the sights in the city when he must have been so very busy trying to learn his part! Of course, he is called at the theater most of the time now, and I feel too fatigued to stroll about as we once did. I need to take a lot of naps, so I stay mostly at Bertramka. I am more profitably engaged there, as a companion and support to my poor dear Madame Dušek. She is in deep mourning for her father, as you know."

"Aaahhh, *La Gran* Bitch Duscecca!"

"You mean *La Granduchessa delle* Bitches, don't you, Teresa?" Both sisters break up laughing and elbowing one another.

"We don't mean to bitch about that bitch, but it's only fair that the Diva is finally brought low after years of queening it over our troupe, but never daring to set foot on a stage with us. Afraid we'd show her up!"

"Not that we don't have sympathy. All us lowly girl musical artistes are all in deep mourning too."

"So-o-o- sad: crying our eyes out! No more Signor Hambacher. No more after-hours trips to The Unicorn House, no more slipping into that stinky old back room, and no more having our names put down in Anton's little black book."

"Maybe Caterina here doesn't mourn so deeply, now that she's got married to Bondini. At least I *think* not, hahaha!"

"Oh, shut your piehole, Teresa! honestly, it's bad enough you tease me about marrying Pasquale for convenience's sake, and you crow in my face about all the prima parts you get, while I'm stuck singing all the 'ina' roles! But in front of Madama Mozart! You don't know who else she talks to, do you?

That's just fucking shitty of you, dear."

"We all have our places in life, Cati; it's not my fault your voice is so small!"

"Excuse me?" says Constanze casually. "Back room? Black Book? Is there a story I'm missing here?"

"Oh, pardon me darling, I guess you wouldn't know about any of *that*. We really shouldn't tell; we don't want to shock you, and it's a sin to tell naughty tales on the dead. But perhaps it might prove useful if you know how things are arranged around here, after all. More wine, please, *ragazzo*, and for my sister too!"

"If you wouldn't mind telling me, perhaps it might help in my husband's case. We all know he was locked in a room with Herr Hambacher's body, but I'm certain he didn't murder him, not even in jest."

"Well, maybe, lots of people say maybe he *did*. He has quite a nasty temper, as we recently saw."

"I know him better than you girls, and he only gets that mad when his singers disappoint him. As you are no doubt aware. But have some more wine, dears, and tell me about Herr Hambacher's 'arrangement.'"

"Well, if you insist, sweetie. We don't want your husband to be hanged! We love him even if he did do a murder!"

"So. Here goes. In case you didn't know, Anton—that is, Signor Hambacher the apothecary—compounds all the high-end *trucco*, the *Geschmink*, the makeup, in the city."

"You mean 'compounDED,' sister, haha!"

"Big, bi-i-g business for him. All the snooty rich bitches slap it on in gobs, and all us theater folk use it too, because it reads well and it doesn't melt off your face and onto your lace—hey, I'm a poet!—as readily as the cheap stuff."

"Really! I had no idea. I just use homemade makeup myself."

"Oh, that's pretty *obvious* to us, dear."

"Plain as the nose on your face, *darling*, ha ha ha!"

"Well, Wolfgang and I have to practice all sorts of economies. Life in Vienna is so very costly, what with high rents, fashionable clothing for appearing at Court, refreshments for entertaining our international celebrity guests and hiring a friseur for when we perform at the great houses where the nobility and even the Emperor attend, and so on. In case you didn't know, many of the great ladies at the Imperial Court have cut back on the amount of paint they wear. Taking their cue from London, I think, where women are going for a more natural, less clownish *commedia dell'arte* look. But you were speaking about the back room and the black book?"

"Well. Thanks for the tip. Save us some money now that...."

"Tell the damn story, sister!"

"Promise not to rat us out? We are all struggling young artistes in this troupe. We have too much work and not enough pay to cover food, housing, and professional expenses. It's easy to come up short, so *we* economize too. But we always need makeup and stage clothes. When some girls run out of cash, they can go to the apothecary's after closing, and Anton lets them into his compounding room and then they ask him for the 'Artist's Discount;' that is, free stuff, if they would let him—do things—to them," whispers Caterina.

"He liked to keep a record," says Teresa, "so he wrote their names down, plus 'everything else,' that happened, right there in his black ledger book. I suppose every girl in the music or theater world, and I'm guessing every poor but noble widow, haha! has gone into that room, one time or another. Except, of course, The Queen of Bitches Josefina Duscecca! And probably that Other Bitch. They get it for free, haha!"

"So—what you're telling me is...

"*Delle vecchie fa conquista, pel piacer di porle in lista*, hahaha!"

"*Voi sapete quel che fa*, hahahahaha!"

"Have some more wine. Did any of his customers, ah, object...to having to pay for their makeup in this way?"

"Geez, who knows? We're sisters, we share all our little secrets, and since we've told you, now you're like our sister too! Kiss-kiss!"

"Mwa-mwa! Mum's the word, unless you want to spill the beans to Her Majesty Josefina the Tsarina! We'd like to see her reaction to *that* bit of news! But Nobody else will ever say anything about how they feel about the good old Artists' Discount."

"But you could ask...you know...*her*."

"Her?"

"The one he patronized, you know her. That other bitch, the one who's not us."

"No skanky old back room for that one, lucky her. Anton was the one paying her salary and giving her whatever she wanted. Full freight. He had some flowery fucknest somewhere out of town where they say he would take her to get her away from, you know...."

"The mother."

"Ah."

"She's killer ambitious, that one. She goes around boasting that this crazy *zingara* gypsy across the river read her cards and told her she would soon be singing at a royal court. Her mother tells the same tale to everyone, *over* and *over*. The bitch is always after Casonova to write letters of introduction to all the impresarios and chancellors and kings he knows, in her behalf. I'm sure he takes full advantage, and promises her the moon, then gives her the sausage, haha. She must be planning for her big audition tour, after this show, we suppose."

"Horseshit Caterina, it's all a scam. I went to that same gypsy myself; she told me I would live to be 106 years old! And still singing! That's one crazy gypsy, Hahaha! You'd believe anybody who tells you something good about career advancement!"

"*Stai zitto, puttana!*"

"*No, stai zitto tu, cortigiana!*"

"*Testa di cazzo!*"

"*Faccia di culo!*"

Constanze, her mind a maelstrom of new and interesting thoughts, tunes out the bickering sisters and thinks she might like to go and see that gypsy as well, to ask if there were hope for her child's survival. She does not say this but ponders many things in her heart as she judiciously sips her wine.

It was intended for the 24, but the illness of one of the female singers caused a new delay…since the company is so small, the impresario is always in a state of anxiety and has to spare his people…my opera will be performed for the first time next Monday, October 29th.

W.A. Mozart to Gottfried von Jacquin, 1787

Madame Dušek's Big Scena

October 21, 1787

Ah, taci, ingiusto core!

Constanze is alone in the music room at Bertramka, doodling at the clavier and humming a tune, when Josepha staggers through the door, tears streaming down a face drained of color and twisted in anguish.

"AhhhhhHHHHH PERFIDO! DECEITFUL WRETCH AND TRAITOR!"

"Good God, Josepha, what is the matter?" says Constanze, rising from the fortepiano.

Madame Dušek picks up an etched glass vase from a side table and throws it against the wall, where it explodes into a thousand irreparable pieces. She tears off her turban, rips it in half, and stomps on it.

"If I cannot avenge myself, May the wrath of God fall on his soul! May He send lightning onto his spirit and hurl it into the mortal abyss!"

"Whom are you cursing and damning so operatically, Josepha? What has happened? Please, I beg you, put that album of Lieder down! Tossing it out the window will not help, stopstopstop! Come here to me now, just take some water and calm yourself," says Constanze, pouring water from a pitcher into a tumbler and reaching it out to Madame Dušek.

The diva sets the songbook down, gulps the water, bows her head, takes a few shaky breaths, clasps her friend's extended hand, and throws the glass out the window. Constanze prudently takes both her friend's hands and leads her to the divan, drawing her down beside her. She continues to restrain her hands, chafing them gently with her own.

"Tell me."

"He- he betrayed me, he *lied* to me, he's ruined my whole life, and I hate him!" Madame Dušek collapses again in spasms of weeping as Constanze holds and rocks her like a child. Several minutes pass before the terrible cries and sobs subside into gentle weeping and quiet moans.

"No, she whispers, "no, that's not true; I love him still. I can't help myself. He is gone, and my heart still beats for him."

"You mean—take this handkerchief, it's fresh—your departed father, is that right, my dear?"

"*Ach! Perfido!*" Another storm of weeping, leading to a yet longer calm, and a wiping away of all tears and snot with Constanze's hankie.

"What has happened? Can you tell me now, or would you like to rest a while?"

"*Ach*. To take up with that *trash* under my very nose! I mean, I expected that he might have re-married after we finished mourning Mama. I could see his having a discreet affair or two with a woman of his class; that's only natural. He was very closed about those things. But this! This!"

"You know her name?"

"YES!! It's MICELLI!"

"Ah. She's...."

"*An opera singer.*"

"Oh dear. But how do you know it was she?"

"Casanova told me. She's gone. He helped arrange her escape. She and her garlic-stinking witch of a mother have fled the city!

"What's that you say? She's contracted to sing Donna Elvira, she can't just flee the city! Is she coming back? Wolfgang says she's been cooped up with a fever for several days. He's been singing her part until she's recovered."

"Did he ever visit her? No, he didn't. Nobody in the Theater did, for fear of contagion."

"Or the inconvenience of being incarcerated."

"He won't be incarcerated for long. The initial doctor's report on poor Papa has been published. Word of the cause of his demise is all over town. Everyone is saying that poor Papa died of a stroke of the heart during an act of love. *Love!* With that cheap Italian gutter slut? She ran away when he became ill and she left him to die! She and her bitch mother lied about her having a fever to cover their escape, and they cleared out. She killed Papa, and I'm going to kill her."

"Oh heaven help us, who's going to sing Donna Elvira then? But at least now they can't say that Wolfgang is the only sus-…oh dear, sorry. Thinking about the show, how rude of me.

"Now then, let's both take a deep breath and reason this out. Your suspicions of Micelli might be hasty. You yourself mentioned that your dear Papa might have had secret affairs with other women, did you not? Perhaps Casanova is lying. Perhaps Micelli was truly poached by an impresario at one of the royal courts she was always rattling on about. Maybe her sudden exit was all about getting a better-paying position."

"More likely all about her fear of being questioned by the police and having to account for her behavior! Leaving poor Papa alone to die, not having the decency to summon anyone to help him, just locking the door and running away and never telling a soul. Maybe…maybe he could have been revived, maybe he would still be alive! Oh, dear God! I'll find her, I'll take my revenge, I'll *kill* her!"

"Well, maybe one or all of those things. But listen now. I think I might have a way of confirming, or overturning, your assumptions. But I must ask you a personal, a delicate question first. Did you ever see, or hear your Papa mention, a—a private account book he kept?"

"No, never. What are you talking about?"

"A few days ago, I had a lunch date with the Saporiti sisters. I stood them to several drinks, just to loosen their tongues and ask them what they knew anything about, well, anything regarding this tragic death and my husband's troubles with the law. I've been trying to ask the theater people, starting with Bassi, who as usual had nothing to say…and I even interrogated the policemen at the prison when I visited Wolfgang They are obediently looking into the popular but ridiculous Mozart-being locked-up-with-the-victim-all-night-long-so-he-must-have-killed-him theory, which is where the Count Nostic and the court seems to want them to look. They are searching for the missing key as well.

"Anyway, the lunch. The Saporitis, once the wine had loosened their tongues, began to gossip: first snarking about my sisters, and then about how Casanova put Bassi up to making love to me, and how I had been duped. What a pair of cats they are! I gave as good as I got but I'm not sure they noticed. I ordered more wine. Then they switched to Micelli, and the *Zigeunerin* fortune teller who predicted she would soon sing before royalty...."

"Everyone knows that gypsy. I went to her once, and she said I would die in utter poverty in a garret in Hradčany. Such horseshit. Go on."

"Mind you, they don't like Micelli very much, so I took what they had to say with a pinch of salt. They told me a wild tale about this little ledger at the White Unicorn, with names of artists and other people he, um, liked, and allowed to run a tab at the shop. I have no idea if what they said was remotely true, but if it would ease your mind, we could look go and look for it and see if, you know...."

"We'll go. You and I. Now."

"Don't you want to, ah, straighten up a bit? Change of clothes? Shall I ring for your maid? Josepha?"

Josepha and Constanze at the White Unicorn

October 21, 1787

Madamina, il catalogo è questo

Fifteen minutes later, the grand diva Josepha Dušek having dressed in a fresh outfit and donned a new turban, the horse having been hitched to the cabriolet, the coachman having taken up the reins and the whip, is being driven north, in the company of her friend Constanze Mozart, to the stone bridge across the Vltava, and into the old town square to the apothecary shop at the sign of the White Unicorn.

Neither friend has spoken; Josepha's face is as pale and as rigid as the Commendatore's marble statue.

"Take the horse to the fountain, Jan, we'll meet you there when we are done," Josepha commands her coachman as they descend. She strides into her father's shop, Constanze in tow. The employees and the manager bow to her and inquire how they might assist Madame.

"I'm going into my father's office. I want to see the ledger."

"Oh, Madame, it makes me so sorry, but Herr Hambacher, God rest his soul, never permitted anyone in that room."

"But he is gone now, and I am his heir. I will go in."

Clients waiting for their prescriptions, observing and accurately gauging the emotional temperature of Prague's most famous woman, wheel in unison like a flock of starlings and head for the exit.

"Please Madame, it is not good to be in there; I must please ask you to not."

Dušek swats the man out of her way and attacks the door. It is locked.

"The key. Now."

"Please, Madame, it is lost."

"You are fired. Now, who has the key?"

"The charlady, Madame. She died suddenly a few months ago. A disease of the kidneys, the doctor said."

"I don't give a fig what she died of. If she was buried clutching that key, go dig her up and bring it to me, or I will take this door off its hinges."

"Pardon me, Madame, I believe there might be a spare key on one of the rings in the stockroom."

"Bring it here to me."

Every clerk and compounder turns to stare at the lowliest employee, who takes the hint and scurries to the back room. He sidles back, eyes on the floor, extending a small bunch of keys at the full length of his arm to Madame, murmuring words of apology and distress. Dušek snatches the bunch and does not thank him.

She locates the right key, unlocks the door, and enters the office, followed by Constanze. Shelves full of bottles, packets, and mortars and pestles for grinding minerals, line the walls. There is a powdery haze and a faint smell of vinegar in the air, which they do not notice. Josepha, striding toward the big desk with the bunch of keys still in her hand, stops dead. She picks out a key, not the one she has just used, but another, smaller key. She holds it up to the dusty beam of light coming from a high window.

"This is a key to my summer house," she mutters. "See, our monogram is on the head of it. Only František and Christian, Papa and I have these keys. How does it come to be on this ring?"

"What is happening, Josepha? What have you found?"

"Someone in this shop has a key or keys to my summer house at Bertramka. Remember, where I locked Wolfgang up?"

"I remember pretty well."

"Who has been in my house?"

"And who might have done harm to your Papa, is that what you're thinking? Someone from this shop?"

"Someone besides Wolfgang or František or Christian, or that street bitch?"

"It seems that now they must consider all the employees at the White Unicorn. Keys can be copied, although probably not with the FJD monogram. But I like it when the field widens to include other suspects. The clerks and compounders seem about as likely to be murderers as Wolfgang, don't they? But look, your father had a key to the summer house which has never been found. Could it be this one?"

"I don't know. How did it end up here? I've told you that the door was locked when I took Wolfgang there that evening, and it was locked when I returned that horrible morning. I am mystified."

"Never mind it right now. Let's do what we came in here to do and look for this notorious ledger. It's so dusty and close in here; I don't want to stay long."

Constanze opens some drawers in Herr Hambacher's desk and shuffles through a mess of unused quills, receipts, sausage papers, empty bottles, correspondence, and other detritus, while Josepha turns the key over and over, shaking her head. At last, Constanze reaches far back into a drawer, pushes a spring lock and finds a hidey-hole containing a small leatherbound book. She draws it out and passes it to her friend.

The diva opens it, turning the pages deliberately, slowly, murmuring under her breath, using the summer house key to guide her eyes down the columns. Time passes, pages flutter, the dusty beam of light moves along the wall.

"Every one. Every last Goddamned actress and opera singer, dating back to my childhood. Look here."

"*Osservate, leggete con me!*"

"What?"

"Oh, never mind, something Da Ponte wrote. Isn't this just a list of his regular makeup clients?"

"No."

"I don't know who these women are...."

"His *special* ones. The artists. He brought them in here and had his way with them in exchange for paint. Their names. Then...in this column, what he required them to do, what he did to them, and here...what he gave them."

"He wrote it all down?"

"God, what a bourgeois he was! He kept such precise records of everything! So meticulous, so damned hypocritical! He didn't forbid me to work in the opera world because all singers are whores and not fit company for me. He just wanted to keep me away from the theater! He needed to shield himself, and his filthy little exercise, from any chance discoveries I might make about who the whoremaster was! It's so disgusting!"

"Maybe…maybe it's not true? Maybe he just kept a book of what he wished he could do but never did."

"Did you not tell me today that the Saporitis knew all about it? How could they have known if they hadn't taken part in his filthy games? Look here, you can see what he did to the Saporitis! Both at once! They, or any of these women here may have killed Papa!"

"Is Micelli on the list?"

"Micelli? No."

"Well then, you mustn't kill her, and you can't kill the Saporitis or any of these other women either."

"I don't want to kill them. It's not their fault. And to think I used to dismiss these violations as just the way of the world! I was wrong! Evil is here! It's bad enough that you and I are seeing these artists, helpless, naked, spraddled, defiled, under the judgment of our gaze in all their shame and need.

"I don't judge them. I don't hate them. It's him I hate. Not like earlier; I hate him with a clear, cold hate for his preying on these poor women. Not for love, not for lust, not for pleasure, but for the greatest consummation he could imagine; the act of writing them up in his damned catalogue, like an inventory of his furniture and china. Ough! Let's get out of this bordello. It stinks of rape and grease paint. Why do the women always lose in these vile games?"

"Perhaps someday we might get to win, at least a little. But you know? I just got an idea of how you yourself can win a little now, and a enjoy a bit—two bits, actually—of revenge too, but only if you wish. Let's walk over to the theater. I'll tell you my plan on the way."

* * *

Josepha and Constanze walk quietly down the aisle of the theater, where Mozart is working his cast through the first act finale, closely observed by his librettist Lorenzo Da Ponte (who is sporting a hangover), Casanova (looking mostly dead) and his enraptured police guard, who are nodding their heads and tapping their feet to the rhythms.

The composer is at the keyboard, playing, cueing the performers, and singing Elvira's part in falsetto when Madame Dušek touches his shoulder, slides onto the bench next to him, glances at the short score, and begins to sing along with him,

"*Tutto, tutto gia si sa…Odi il tuon della vendetta, che ti fischia intorno, sul tuo capo in questo giorno il suo fulmine cadrà!*"

The composer having looked at her in surprise, stops singing and lets her take over. The cast onstage glances her way and immediately ups its energy level to match the mighty bell of her voice. The stretto section of the finale takes on a spark of life for the first time and ends in a blaze of glory. The audience, consisting of the aforementioned, the choristers and a dozen stagehands, applauds, stamps its feet, and yells at the top of its lungs.

"Break! Everybody take fifteen minutes," calls the stage manager.

"You weren't kidding about the sight-reading, were you?" says Mozart.

"I'll do it," says Josepha.

"Do what?"

"Micelli does not have a fever, Wolfgang. She has skipped town; she's not coming back, and I am going to sing this role in her place. And you are going to write me a solo *scena*."

"Doesn't she? Has she? Won't she? Will you? Am I? Can you tell me what is happening, please?" begs Wolfgang.

Chief Kretènček marches down the aisle and confers with Mozart's guardians. All three approach the composer. He stares wild-eyed and opens his mouth in song:

> *Are you detaining me again?*
> *Tossing me back into the pen?*
> *Are you in earnest or in jest?*
> *You must have others to arrest!*
> *Three times too many, I protest!*

"Excuse me, Sir Mozart," says the chief, bowing and clicking his heels, "but the official report of the Coroner's Office has finally been issued. We have some few questions to ask you and then we will show you what this report says, if it pleases you, sir."

"I hope your questions are not as ridiculous as the last set, Chief."

"Here we go, sir. Please answer truly. How long had you known Herr Hambacher, the deceased?"

"Never met him. I made a first acquaintance with him when I stepped and pissed on him a fortnight past."

"Ah. Because it says here, let me show you, and your lovely wife and *Verehrte Kammersängerin* Madame Dušek, that the coroner estimates time of death to be somewhere around October 3. It goes on to say that 'Upon the opening of the body it was discovered that Deceased suffered from organ deterioration if not outright organ failure of a chronic nature, including heart, liver and kidney failure consistent with long term poisoning from mercury and lead.'

"Now, according to the registry at the Three Lions, you arrived in Prague on the night of the fourth October, so I don't think you have been in the city long enough to achieve a long-term poison murder of the deceased, do you?"

"I do not."

"Then it's probably not you who did it, is it?"

"It is not."

"Then, dear sir, you are free to move out of the jail."

"Awwwww," groan the guards.

> *But is my release not premature?*
> *I've got to write the overture!*
> *Let me stay a little while*
> *In my happy durance vile!*

The Chief looks helplessly at Constanze.

"Don't worry, he's been talking in verse lately, what with all the *Sturm und Drang* he's been suffering, not least the murder accusation. It'll stop soon. I hope," Constanze murmurs to the Chief.

"What I mean is, says Mozart, lapsing into prose, "I'm not leaving jail yet, because I have yet to fulfill our dear bereaved noble patron's request for an overture for this accursed skit; and I would like to follow his command that I remain incarcerated until I do. It's the least I can do for him after his tragic loss.

Besides, I need peace and quiet with no distractions to write a big fire-breathing *scena* for Donna Elvira, as this dear lady has commanded me. Yes, she has joined the cast. *Then* I'll go, but not before. I have my honor, you know. Besides, we need to rehearse the Brotherhood of Policemen cantata."

"Excuse me, dear Chief," murmurs Josepha, drawing that good man a little aside. "Is there any mention of a key with the Bertramka monogram FJD on it being found during the closer examination of my dear Papa?"

"Madame, there was never a key among his personal effects. And the door to the scene of the crime was open with a key in the outer keyhole when we arrived, as you know."

"My own key. You have it in evidence, I believe. And here is a key I have recently removed from my father's ring at the White Unicorn. I believe it is his. How did it get there, I wonder. Do you?"

"I do wonder, surely, dear Madame, and I condole your loss. I will look into it."

The Stage Manager calls all the participants to their places, and the rehearsal re-starts. Josepha takes her seat beside Mozart to sight-read from the top of another run-through of the Act I Finale.

* * *

That evening, Mozart, Constanze, and his loyal escort return to Police House. Inflamed and horrified by the tale his dear wife tells him about her and Josepha's activities earlier in the day, he requests use of the guardroom for the whole night, tunes his little clavichord, and writes Donna Elvira's recitative and rondo "In quali eccessi o numi/Mi tradí," all in one go.

For those of you, dear readers, who will insist that this aria was written for Katharina Cavalieri for Don Giovanni's revival in Vienna the following spring, the author can only refer you to a letter Mozart wrote to his friend Gottfried von Jacquin about "another aria" that he wrote in Prague, which he regretted not being able to send to him right away. Since Mozart's Prague catalog only records Josepha's concert aria "Bella mia fiamma," we can only assume that the story set forth here, of how "Mi tradì" came to be written, and how Madame Dušek finally made her operatic debut is, possibly, conceivably, as true as any other. Trust the author on this, as in all things she tells you.

Constanze and Josepha Pay a Visit to Casanova

Count Waldstein's town house, October 21, 1878

Ah, chi mi dice mai quell barbaro dov'è?

The same evening that Mozart is writing "Mi tradì," Josepha Dušek and Constanze Mozart pay a call on Giacomo Casanova at Count Waldstein's town residence in Malá Strana. They are on a fact-finding mission concerning the doings of the runaway soprano Caterina Micelli, who may or may not have murdered Herr Hambacher, but who may have left him dying or dead for a number of hours, or days. Lorenzo Da Ponte, being out on a date with Saporiti, is not present at the interview.

When the two women are seated and offered refreshment, Josepha informs Casanova of the purpose of their visit: namely, to find out what role he might have been playing in the sudden disappearance of the lady contracted to sing the role of Donna Elvira in the world premiere of *Don Giovanni*, and what he might know about the tragic death of her father.

"Well, dear ladies, you know this story in part. Now, at your command I am duty-bound to confess all."

"You have our complete attention."

"Of course, as you might have guessed, it was I who killed your father. No, seat yourselves please, and allow me to continue.

"I did so in my own defense, as he was doing his very best to kill me! Madame Dušek, *La Grande* Duskovà, queen of musical Prague! Shall I tell your fortune? I heard you sing a few months ago at a private concert and I was thrilled! I fell instantly, hopelessly, in love with you! Such fire, such sensibility, such seductive roulades spinning from your luscious mouth!

"I immediately wrote to you, in all friendship, begging for a meeting. You were amused, even intrigued, that a man of my years and diminished position in life would have the temerity to approach you. You were fascinated by rumors of my international travels, my great learning, my many death-defying adventures, my friendship with kings, popes, and princes; perhaps you had even heard stories of my countless liaisons with women of quality; or no quality, or nuns, or little girls and boys. The tales are all true, and all to be published in my memoirs, which I am now writing. You will be in there too, dear lady; if death spares me for that long.

"You were above all, if I may say so, sexually curious. You wanted to sate that curiosity; you freely admitted it. You are stuck in the aging woman's dilemma: you are too young to forego sex, and too old to attract lovers. Your husband is elderly and has always preferred men. Your younger lover, the handsome and talented Count Clam, is growing weary of you, and has probably reached that state where he laments aloud that he is not worthy of your love; which always means he is bored and wants to feast on fresher meat. You envy his freedom to do so; why should he have this privilege when you do not? We are living in an Enlightened Age, where all of humankind can challenge the old rules and restrictions and claim ownership of our desires. Why should you not follow this new path, out of curiosity or lust, or desperation, or even ennui? We agreed on an assignation. We had one, and several more.

"However, my body and soul really wanted to fuck you, dear lady. At my advanced age, I feared not being up to the task of entering you and sustaining the act of love. I decided to buy some insurance to make the process run more reliably. Hence, I repaired to the apothecary's in the Town Square, with the purpose of purchasing some assurance caps, just in case; and principally to request the compounding of a little aphrodisiac potion of my own devising; and some potency powder, ditto, for myself.

"I was welcomed by an assistant, and I introduced myself as the archivist in the service of Count Waldstein. From then on, I was served by the head apothecary himself, who supplies my noble employer with various over-priced, useless nostrums and love aids. I had never been in the shop, but the dear Count's name and spending habits got me all the attention I wanted.

"He brought me some sheepskin assurance caps, which I duly inflated with my breath to check for leaks. In due time, I drew him aside and asked him to be so kind as to compound the scrips I gave him, since I was about to embark on an amorous adventure. He seemed more than interested, winking and silently nodding his understanding. Perceiving that I had a sympathetic ear, I began to boast about my new conquest: a magnificent artiste, nay, the pillar in the musical life of her city, and perhaps in all the Empire. A fine soprano and keyboard player, a philanthropist, endowed with beauty, passion and womanly delicacy thrown into the bargain. I needed those amorous aids, because I was sure her appetites are as wanton and fierce as her singing. He kept nodding and winking in a brotherly, conspiratorial sort of way; he said he would compound the scrips himself and that they would be ready in one day.

"I sent a note to my lover—that would of course be you—who agreed to meet me in a summer house in the vineyard on her estate after dark on a given evening. She informed me that there is a back way into the estate, that the laborers use, the gate of which stood open for the harvest that was just completed, and for the tending of the vines in preparation for winter.

"When I duly arrived the next day to pick up my love potions. An assistant brought them to me and I examined them, as I always do. I can tell if these love-philtres are correctly compounded by my superb sense of smell. It is my strongest and most infallible sense, followed closely by touch. I can remember what all my women smelled like; their perfumes, their sweat, their hair, their blood issue, the musky love-juices that oozed from them into my enraptured nose and mouth. Each one different, each wonderful, voluptuous, intoxicating. I'm getting semi-erect now, just thinking about them.

"I opened the packet containing my virility potion, and I knew instantly that the compounding was wrong. Not only wrong, but deadly. Instead of predominant notes of dried ram's testicle, which carries a whiff of lanolin and ripe cheese, this concoction reeked of marzipan and mycelium! Somebody had insinuated arsenic and a decoction of *amanita phalloides*—oh, the irony!—into this powder. The apothecary! I withdrew from the shop. I was furious, and wanted to kill him then and there, but no. I decided to find out something about him and his strange murderous motives first.

"I consulted with the opera troupe, which of course knows everything about everybody, since they move in circles both high and low in the city. More particularly, I consulted Bassi, whom I had been tutoring in my fool-proof seduction techniques to use in his new role as Don Juan. He is engaged in a flirtation, at my suggestion and with my coaching, with a delightful little matron who has a lot of free time in the city, and succeeding splendidly, if I do say so."

"Yes," says Constanze, "Luigi was very charming and attentive; congratulations to you both. I was flattered and touched by his efforts at seduction, I admit it. But my chastity remains unmovable as a rock."

"My dear Madame Mozart, I am so disappointed in you. I am sure your famous husband has had his chances, and taken them, too. Why not you as well? Who would blame you? Where is your sense of adventure? *Pace, pace*! Don't spoil your lovely brows with such a glare as that. And uncurl your sweet lips; that grimace is so unattractive. Surely you must have thrilled to the idea of having a pretty boy barely out of his teens as a lover. Surely you will confess that you were contemplating lifting your skirts and spreading your knees for him, please say you were; I would be personally so hurt if you were not."

"Never mind that right now," says Josepha. "I want to hear rest of the story of this old scoundrel spins about my Papa."

"Cherished Madame, your every wish.... I duly consulted with the ambrosial Signor Bassi, and he dropped the bomb. He told me you were the apothecary's daughter. Oh! how could I have been so careless, Madame, as to have told your father all my tender hopes and dreams regarding the lady whom he must have recognized as his beloved child? Truly I meant no harm to you, no harm in the world! I meant to delight you, and I did, insofar as I was able! Yet here was your Papa trying to poison me before I could transport you to even higher realms of bliss! This was an insult not to be borne! I was determined to be avenged!

"I set about making up a long list of expensive love-potions, of a particularly useless but costly nature, to be delivered in person by Herr Hambacher himself, to me, Count Waldstein's agent. The Count, I wrote, was coming to town for the wedding gala and wanted to visit his favorite places of amusement. Who could refuse such a lucrative order, even from one's intended murder victim?

"In two days, your father came up to Waldstein's town house in Malá Strana with bundles and packets bulging his pockets. He was breathing hard and sweating when I greeted him and asked him if he would come to my rooms and take some refreshment after climbing up the hill. I set before him, and before myself, large glasses of wine. His glass contained his own recipe of arsenic and mushrooms he had made specially for me. The good apothecary duly drank a large draught and promptly died. I engaged a couple of thugs to bundle the body into a handcart and deliver it under cover of night and under my supervision, over to Betramka and through the aforementioned vineyard gate to the summer house. I picked the lock and my assistants bundled him inside, where you, Madame, were sure to find it. Perhaps on the day before our agreed-upon assignation was to take place, perhaps sooner. I used the picks to lock the door again. I am quite coolly meticulous when I'm avenging myself."

The two women sat rigidly upright with narrowed eyes and tightened lips during this gleeful tale of vendetta. Finally, after a long and increasingly tense silence, Josepha spoke.

"This is…the most astounding confession I have ever heard in my life."

"Thank you, Madame."

"It is, or at least the vendetta portion of it is, the biggest pile of steaming horseshit, the most outrageous collection of lies, fantasies, garbage, offal, and evil I have ever heard.

"How do I know? Did you think an apothecary's daughter would not see the holes in your vaunted knowledge of toxins? That I wouldn't know that arsenic and amanita have no discernible scents? That arsenical poisoning—even from a large dose—would take hours? And that amanita poisoning might take several days? Prussic acid would kill instantly, and it smells of almonds, but you were careless and conflated one poison with another in your silly mendacious tale.

"And do you think Madame Mozart and I are not aware of the condition in which my poor Papa's body was found? Both she and I have read the coroner's report, and we know what he was doing when he died, and with whom, and why he died. Why are you shielding the woman?"

"Ah, I surrender! You have caught me out, clever ladies. As for Signorina Micelli.…"

"Aha! so it was Signorina Micelli!" cried Constanze. "We thought so, but we were not entirely sure."

"You think entirely too much, Madame Mozart. Overuse of the female brain may cause the fetus to wither in the womb, you know."

"Ach! I…You.…"

"As for Signorina Micelli and her hasty departure from Prague—you wily minxes! I will now tell you the whole truth."

"If that is within your power, please proceed."

"It is. I have nothing to lose by it, but it won't be as exciting a yarn as the one I made up. That tale is novelistic! Coruscating! Brilliant! I'm definitely putting it in my memoir!

"*Ebbene.* La Micelli was convinced that a career at court was in her future. She was hounding me to write letters to my noble and royal acquaintances in all the major cities I have been thrown out of: Paris, Berlin, Moscow, Venice, Madrid. She said she could suck the audition tour money out of silly old Hambacher, who was obsessed with her and who was paying her keep, as well as her salary, to the late unlamented Countess Nostic."

"That's another lie!" cries Josepha.

"Look in the back of the ledger," murmurs Constanze, "on the debit side. We never looked there before. There they are, the late Countess and Micelli both."

"Perhaps the poor man really loved her.…"

"It seems so, in this instance."

"Let me finish, dear ladies! After Micelli's unfortunate tryst with your Papa at Bertramka, she kept mum and waited a while to see how the case would play out. As long as Mozart was the prime suspect, she felt reasonably safe; but when the Saporiti sisters started to speculate and insinuate, and the coroner issued his findings, Micelli knew the cat was going to come out of the bag. She had played her cards badly; she had panicked and abandoned a dying man— who, moreover, was her chief underwriter at the theater—without bothering to help him or to summon those who could. She needed to leave Prague, *Don Giovanni* world premiere or no.

"She came to me and begged me to help her get out of town. I told her to go to her rooms, write a note that she had a contagious disease, and nobody should come near her. She should stay hidden and wait for me to arrange transportation and letters of introduction for her. These things I did. Micelli and her mother are now in Germany waiting upon my friend Count

Hasenpfeffer, a generous patron of the arts with an eye for a pretty young woman. I am sure she will get a hearing in Berlin."

"But the key to my summer house...?"

"Surely you can puzzle that out, dear Josepha. Micelli, for all her panicked leave-taking, kept a cool head about the key. She took it from the inside lock and secured the door behind her. She gave that key to me, and I hung it on the doorknob of the Unicorn one evening late. One of the clerks must have taken it, all unknowing, or perhaps all-knowing, and put it on your Papa's ring. Do you think your Papa's loyal employees are unaware of his doings? They would never spill the beans while he was living, but they may do so now that he is gone. See to it that they don't."

"Speaking of going," says Constanze, "it is late and we must be taking our leave. We have a *Sitzprobe* to attend tomorrow. Madame Dušek will be singing the entire role of Donna Elvira with orchestra, for the first time."

"Not true sight-singing, though," says Josepha. "I had a glance at it earlier. Everything will go smoothly."

"Addio, my Sirens, my Circes. You are so ravishing when you are angry. Are you sure you won't stay and keep an old man company? No? What wondrous women you are!"

"We really cannot bear to stay any longer, Chevalier."

"As you wish. But you, Constanze Mozart, you don't deserve to play second fiddle to your husband! You are brilliant! Live your life as you will! Take it by the horns, or by the membrum, and seek your pleasure!"

The two women are shown out. They climb back into their conveyance and head for Bertramka.

"Whew!" says Constanze, "I feel as if I need several vinegar baths just to get minimally clean. What a filthy old man."

"Maybe we should both jump into the river to shrive ourselves. Ugh! And to think I had so much fun with him! I am really confused about filthy old men. I go round and round, over and over, so it seems."

The Overture

Prague Police House, October 26

Vedrai, carino

On his penultimate evening in jail, the towering genius Mozart sets himself to writing the overture to *Don Giovanni*. He economizes a bit by using material from the grand finale as an introduction, and then writes a clever, high-contrast little development that doesn't end, but slithers right into the action of the first scene. He is very pleased with it and sends the full score out first thing in the morning to the copyist to make the parts.

At the same time, the man who will play Don Giovanni—the lovely Luigi Bassi—sends a message by courier to Constanze at Bertramka, begging her to meet him privately in his rooms by the right bank of the river, that humble quarter where stevedores toil and artists and other poor folk reside. He must tell her things that will directly affect her husband, the fate of the opera, and much, much more. He will meet her at the Bridge Tower and escort her there, incognito. If she would do the same and hide her face, it would be good. She sends a return reply, stating the hour and confirming the place, and the manner of her disguise.

They meet, cloaked and hooded, half-hidden in the autumn mists, before the East tower of the Bridge, and walk to his dwelling. They sit opposite each other on either side of the tiny stove, where a few coals are still glowing, and gaze once more at each other for many minutes.

"Thank you so much for agreeing to see me, Madame Mozart. I am in such pain."

"How do you mean? Are you going to pantomime your undying adoration for me again?"

"No, not anymore, Madame. First, I must confess that I do not really love you, or not very much anyway. It was Casanova's idea for me to pay attention to you so you would get Signor Mozart to write a proper *scena* for me."

"I guessed that. I really don't love you very much either, but I suppose we were both playing the same game of flirtation, were we not? You wanted an aria, and I wanted someone to talk to. Or at. It's so nice to have a companion who listens, and who is not in jail. Shame on us both, I guess, but that's water under the bridge. So, what is the cause of your pain this time?"

"I have a terrible confession to make, I cannot bear it alone any longer."

"My dear young man, pardon me; I see you really are in distress. What troubles you?"

"I wanted to kill Signor Mozart."

"As have many, including me. Oh dear, I see you are also deadly serious. Was it this whole *scena* business?"

"Yes. No. It was when he shamed me in front of the cast and treated me like a child. I'm not a child! I am a grown man and I have a man's feelings, and a man's honor. I challenged him to a duel too, first with swords and then with guns, and he mocked at me and got me all confused until I agreed to a duel over billiards. I don't even play billiards."

"He does."

"Yes, I know. So, I went up onstage like a whipped dog when he ordered me to, and sang that cursed wine aria—badly—and everybody was looking at me and laughing. I never felt so small in my life. I woke up in the middle of the night in a rage, and all my desire to kill your husband returned in full force. I decided I must do it, but how?"

"Oh you poor dear, it's not your fault. You were the victim of my husband's perverse mood. He is usually so happy, genuinely happy, even when the pressures of his life seem almost unbearable. He has always loved his colleagues; always helped them and encouraged them to be at their best. But...let me explain a bit. Since my husband's Papa died in May, he has been possessed by dark demons raging inside him, and nothing I can do will exorcise them. Because I am a part of his possession, you see. His Papa despised me, and his sister has been exceedingly hateful to both of us. The Mozart family used to be so close-knit. I know how shattered and guilt-ridden Wolfgang was when his Mama died in his care in Paris, because he has confessed that to me. But it's more complicated this time. Not a word has he uttered about his Papa, about how he both hated and loved him, about how he is not allowing himself to grieve for him. You see?

"My husband must feel, somewhere inside himself, that I was the intruder who estranged him from his Papa and sister; even though he defied their wishes and married me. But the agony of the loss of their affection eats at his heart. He still loves me, I don't doubt it, and I love him. But he is just…harder, darker now, and I am not the one who can help him heal. You understand? You will have noticed that he is not the same merry little man he was when he conducted you in *Figaro*."

"Yes, I have noticed. It hurts that he is so mean to me."

"That makes me so sorry, Luigi. But on a more practical note, you must have realized that if you killed Wolfgang, he would definitely not have written you an aria? That's his firm policy, you know."

"Really? I never thought about that at all, I was so furious."

"So, is that all that's bothering you? Your murderous fancies?"

"No, Madame, that is only the beginning."

"Tell me the middle now."

"I. I bought a gun. The kind Signor Mozart used to shoot. That's the only kind I know about. I got it from a wild-game hunter who sells to our troupe's favorite restaurant. I bought some bullets also. I asked the man to teach me how to shoot. So he showed me how to stand and how to aim and how to fill the air chamber.

"I shot a few times, and shooting the gun made me feel much better, although I missed the target. I went back to the theater because now I was late for my call. I went in and stashed the gun in the properties cabinet. There are lots of fake guns in there, and probably nobody would notice a real one among them."

"You were still angry, and now you had the power of vendetta in your grasp, didn't you, Luigi?"

"Yes. I wasn't going to let anybody shame me ever again."

"Is that the end of your tale, then?"

"Yes. No. I can't."

"It's hard, I know, but…if you keep this story inside yourself, the demons will eat you alive, just as they eat my husband. You know this. It's already happening."

"But—to you...."

"You sought me out, did you not? I want to protect my husband, but I also want to help you. Our flirtation is over but something like a friendship begins between us, I think. Where is your gun now, Luigi?"

"In the Vltava. I threw it in there. Because it was so terrible."

"What was? Tell me the end now, and you will feel better. I feel better already, trust me. I won't betray you."

"I pictured shooting your husband in the middle of rehearsals, after I sing 'Metà di voi,' when I take Masetto's gun. I was going to switch out the prop gun for my real gun at the last moment, and Masetto would bring it onstage without knowing anything about it. I imagined I would not beat Masetto with my gun but turn downstage and shoot Signor Mozart in front of everyone, so they would see that I am a man, not a little helpless boy. The picture in my mind got so strong that, after we the night we played *Figaro*, I hid in the theater, so I could rehearse my vendetta scene onstage. I got my gun out of the cabinet from amongst the others and prepared it. I felt stronger and stronger all the while I was doing this. I was my own man, a man of honor, a man of action!

"I went onto the stage. There was moonlight and starlight from the windows, which were opened to air out the house after the show. I crossed stage right. I was the hunter now, and he was the hunted."

"*E sono assalitore d'assalito.*"

"That's from the show, isn't it?"

"Yes, Donna Anna sings it in Act I. I changed it to be a man, like you, though."

"I acted out aiming my rifle at the clavier, where the maestro sits. I imagined what I would say to him right before I killed him. Then something. ..."

"Please go on. I understand you."

"There was a noise in the Estates Box, like barking or howling, a terrible noise like a werewolf or a demon from hell come to fetch me. I turned around very fast, the barrel of the rifle hit the proscenium, and it went off. I heard the ball hit something. There was another horrible scream and then it was all quiet. I knew I had hit a person in the box! How could I have hit anybody? I can't even aim right!"

"Beginner's luck, I suppose."

"I am so sorry, God forgive me, I killed her, I didn't mean to kill her, I didn't really mean to kill Signor Mozart either; it was so horrible to kill a living soul."

"There, there. Here's my handkerchief. Hold onto my hands. Take some slow breaths. Let me talk for a minute. Listen to what I say.

"You fell down on the stage, and you wept for what you had been imagining, and what you did, even by accident, didn't you? That shows you are still good at heart. Yes?"

"I don't know."

"And then you left the theater, and you ran through the streets to the river. You thought of throwing yourself in along with the rifle, didn't you? Of course you did. But then, there would no *Don Giovanni*, no career, no fame, no life, no love. Maybe if you could just keep it all a secret you could have that wonderful future, Isn't that right?"

"Yes. There is still more. I'm in your power now, so I might as well tell."

"Tell."

"When the police questioned us, all of us, many people who work in the theater mentioned that they had heard Signor Mozart boasting to me about being a crack shot and shooting people he hated between the eyes. I know that's really not what he said, but I...I mentioned this to the police also.

"The police thought that Signor Mozart had a very good alibi, being under lock and key after the show. Then some other people mentioned that they had seen him pointing his finger at the Countess and threatening to kill her. Pointing the finger at somebody in the Bohemian Lands means you are laying a curse on them. Theater people already believed that Signor Mozart had signed a contract with the Devil, especially after they heard the graveyard scene and the grand finale when the Stone Father comes to dinner. It scared them. They think Signor Mozart used witchcraft to escape the jail, or to shoot the countess while he was still locked up. When the police asked me if I also held this opinion, I said yes, I did. But I don't believe it. Oh God, I lied, I sinned. I am going to hell. Now the stone father will come for me, I know he will."

"Where is your father, Luigi?"

"Dead. My mother too. I was raised by the priests in the Santa Maria Cathedral choir college in Pesaro."

"Were the fathers kind to you?"

"Yes. No. Sometimes…they did bad things to me."

"Go ahead and weep, dear fellow," says Constanze, stroking the young man's hair and kissing away his tears. "You have made a terrible mistake, and I can see how sorry you are. You're still young, with a good life ahead of you, so perhaps we can still make things right. But this calls for more repentance and sacrifice on your part."

"I know. Don't stop kissing me. Hold me. I am so alone."

There are many fanciful legends about the writing of the overture to Don Giovanni, and I am delighted to muddy the waters even further for you. Some sources will tell you that Mozart was drinking with his buddies the night of October 28 and wrote the overture in the wee hours of the 29, with Constanze keeping him awake by telling him stories; that he presented it to the copyists who worked like dogs all day to have it ready by the time the audience was gathered.

Others, including Mozart, claim he completed his work on the 28. It is rumored that he wrote out the parts without a master score (since he was going to conduct from memory), and had a copyist duplicate them on the same day. The orchestra may or may not have sight-read the piece perfectly, provoking a riotous ovation. But this bit is subject to suspicion, because there is no space for an ovation, since the overture transitions directly into the opening scene.

How many rehearsals did an orchestra usually get before performing a new piece in those days? Zero. They were expected to sight-read things, for good or ill. Since it didn't much matter when the Prague city orchestra laid eyes on the overture, you may have noticed that the author slyly front-loaded the wee-hours-and- Constanze's story-telling-to-keep-him-awake legend, the better for Mozart to play a practical joke on Casanova. Believe me, Mozart wrote the overture in jail.

Count Nostic and Mozart and Constanze and Da Ponte and Casanova

October 27, 1787

Di rider finirai pria dell'aurora!

The copyists for the theater, working in a fever, have finished all the parts to the overture to *Don Giovanni*. They have returned them to the jail, where the towering genius Mozart reviews them before sending them on Herr Strobach to distribute to his orchestra before the final dress rehearsal, where they will be reading it at sight. In the audience at this momentous rehearsal are Constanze, František Dušek, Count Clams, Giacomo Casanova, Lorenzo Da Ponte and certain wealthy patrons getting a privileged sneak peek; plus the Chief of Prague police Kretènček, Constable Jiří Pospíšil and as many members of the law enforcement personnel as can be spared from their duties. Absent are Count Nostic, who is grieving, and Anton Hambacher, who is dead, and perhaps rolling over in his grave at the thought of his daughter's making her operatic debut. Or perhaps not, since he has his own manifold sins and wickednesses to consider as he awaits the day of judgment in that narrow house. As do we all.

The evening is a wild success. The orchestra plays the overture without a mistake to be heard, Josepha Dušek sings the role of Donna Elvira off book with credible *mis-en-scène*. The cast, not to be outdone, sings the difficult music with brio and conviction; especially brilliant is the young Luigi Bassi, who brings a dashing, yet haunted quality to his character, especially in the final scene where he defies God and is dragged to hell by a chorus of demons arriving and departing through a trapdoor in the stage.

* * *

After a small celebration at the Theater, Mozart and Constanze and their loyal guardians walk to the jail, where the couple are embraced by everyone in a tearful farewell. Mozart promises to continue rehearsing the policemen's cantata, and the good Chief vows to find a performance venue for its world premiere, before the run of *Don Giovanni* is over. Josepha has gone home ahead, to rest up for her début. The Mozarts pack up Wolfgang's belongings, including his pipe. A carriage is waiting to receive the luggage and the couple and take them back to Bertramka. The doors of the Prague central police station close behind the Mozarts, for the last—hopefully the last—time.

No sooner have the couple left the building when Wolfgang is knocked to the ground by a dark figure lunging out of the shadows, roaring a battle yell. It is Count Nostic, standing over Mozart, slashing the air with a Polish cavalry saber and brandishing a knife in his other hand.

The composer rolls under the carriage away from his assailant, screams for help, leaps to his feet and runs for his life. He careens through a narrow back alley, looking for an open door, with Nostic charging along behind, panting and cursing and beating his sword on the closed shutters of the houses. Behind them lumbers Constanze, shrieking for the police, or anybody, to stop the mayhem. Alas, the nearest policemen, having gathered to bid farewell to their beloved composer, are now all in the guardroom having a solemn and consoling drink of beer…

Mozart sees the arch of the old East Tower, the entrance to the stone bridge, and, terrified to meet the old soldier in the open on the span, veers to the right and takes a set of slimy stone stairs down to the river-front, where the warren of warehouses, docks, brothels and tenement slums might serve to hide him. Ducking into the first brothel he encounters, he crashes into Da Ponte and Casanova, who are just leaving.

"Nostic is trying to kill me."

The two Venetians, one ancient and the other infirm, find a reserve of strength in this time of need. They spin Mozart around, grab him by the elbows, and lift him half-off his feet. They hustle him through the precincts of the establishment and out the back door, down another flight of stairs onto the riverbank mud. The three men stagger several yards before they stumble over an exposed sewer outlet-pipe, disturbing the peace of the local rats squealing and scrabbling to get out of their way. They thrash around in the muck, right themselves, and make their way around a dark warehouse to a lantern-lit loading dock and thence to a timber raft where a rough gang of stevedores is offloading barrels.

"This is Mozart," says Da Ponte to one of the stevedores. "Somebody is trying to kill him. Hide him somewhere."

"Really, you're shitting me, that's Mozart? The guy who wrote 'Non più andrai?' Fuck me, it IS him! Get him on board, and put him back there behind those barrels. Take out your hooks, boys, and keep your eyes peeled for any son of a whore who wants to hurt this guy! Whoever it is, rip his guts out if he comes near here!"

Mozart, Casanova and Da Ponte find themselves squatting behind some leaking barrels of rock salt that have just made the dangerous journey down the Vltava from the southern mines.

"Well, here we all are," whispers Da Ponte, "covered in mud and rat shit, salted like hams and perched on wet logs on the shore of a river which is slowly soaking into our garments; free from imprisonment, but on the lam from our murderous noble patron. What could be more fun?"

"Breaking out of jail," murmurs Casanova.

* * *

Constanze almost crashes into Count Franz-Anton Nostic as he stands in the dimly-lit street between a brothel on the left and a moldering tenement house on the right, peering into the darkness.

"Stop this mad errand, at once!" she commands him. As he whirls to challenge her, she lays a firm and gentle hand on his sword arm.

"Put your sword in its place. My husband is innocent. I know who killed your wife."

Nostic Speaks

October 27, 1787

Dalla sua Pace la mia dipende

A half-hour later, Count Nostic and Constanze are sitting in front of a majolica stove in a small parlor in his palace on the left bank, in Malá Strana. He is slumped in his chair, exhausted, devastated, but alert. Constanze, sitting erect and leaning a little towards him, has been speaking to him for some time in a low and confidential tone.

"There is no happy end to this story. The shooting was an accident; such a stupid, unlikely, tragic accident for you, for all of us. I don't know what you should do with Bassi. The poor young man was acting out a fantastical plot to work the shooting of my husband into his performance at the dress rehearsal, but I have no idea if he would have actually gone through with it. Wolfgang did use him very badly, humiliating him in front of his colleagues, and refusing to write him the solo *scena* he wanted so much. I believe my husband's public shaming of young Bassi awoke some unhappy childhood events in his mind, sending him off into a fit of blind rage. He's suffering agonies of remorse right now, but the rage is past. He seems to be a nice enough young man—too much under the influence of Casanova perhaps—but with a good heart.

"Unfortunately, Wolfgang also has been re-visiting unhappy memories from his own childhood ever since the death of his Papa. He too has expressed his own rage in all kinds of unfortunate ways, hurting the innocent people around him, including Bassi. His rage and Bassi's collided and exploded, setting off the events that led to the Countess's tragic but unintended death. I am so sorry."

"He killed her," says Nostic. "He must pay. He must be brought to the law, and he must confess."

"Yes, he must. But he didn't mean to kill her; he only wanted to kill my husband. And, may I remind you, so did *you*. In that light, I think you might have some fellow-feeling for the poor boy, and even forgive him eventually, dear Count."

"I *did* want to kill Mozart. I thought he had escaped from jail and murdered my wife as he had publicly threatened to do. I was mad with grief. I followed him for several nights, but there was always the police guard alongside him. But I shouldn't use my murderous mania as an excuse for my actions, because, you know, I didn't seriously attempt to kill him until Strobach had the overture from him. That shows that I was perhaps more calculating than crazy."

"But now, Count, I want to ask you, if you can bear to speak of it; why was the late Countess still in her box so late at night? Why did she not come back with you to this house after the performance of *Figaro*?"

"My poor MariLise. She has suffered so terribly these past few years. My peace of mind has always depended upon hers, and I tried to ease her pain as much as I could. I tried to keep up the appearance that all was well with her. I tried to stand between her and the tattletales of society. But to answer your question; she asked me if she could be alone for a few hours, to avoid meeting anybody."

"What happened that the Countess needed to hide, may I ask?"

"It's complicated. Let me try to explain. The final straw was the cruel snub dealt to her—the leading noblewoman of Prague!—by the royal couple, who were her guests in the Estates Box. They left abruptly without acknowledging her; but they told others on their way out, *and in her hearing*, that they could not bear to stay any longer because 'she smelled like a dog.' This outrageous insult was passed around the theater and everyone had heard it before the fourth act began. It was impossible for her to face Prague society after that. So she hid."

"How terrible for her."

"The penultimate straw was, of course, being bested in the fight with your husband over the *Figaro* performance and being insulted and threatened by him in front of the cast and crew and Count Le Noble."

"That was inexcusable. I apologize on his wretched little behalf."

"All that my poor MariLise had left in her life was her exalted rank. Which rank, alas, she flaunted in the faces of her friends and all of society in an indelicate, often harsh, fashion. But she didn't realize she was putting everybody off; her mind was going."

"I am so, so sorry, dear Count. If Wolfgang had only known…if they had met under less stressful circumstances.…"

"I loved her so much. You should have known her in the old days when we first married. She was lovely, so sweet and kind to high and low. She had locks of glossy chestnut hair and a beautiful smile. Her voice.…"

"Please take a moment. I understand."

"Her voice. She used to sing like a nightingale. Only at private events of course, but she was in demand at parties and balls. But she loved the theater, and that was what brought us together, our love of opera and plays. She had a considerable role in founding the National Theater, and she loved it like her favorite child. We stayed up late many a night together after shows in that cursed box—so blessed in those days—talking over what we had seen and heard on the stage, discussing how we could make things better for those who labored in that house, and those who came to see our productions. We talked about which celebrated artists we could entice to Prague, including, of course, Herr Mozart. Elizabeth was a true partner for me, until her decline began. She.…"

"My dear Count, I understand how painful this is for you. If you wish to say more, I will listen with my whole heart."

"She lost her teeth. That is not so unusual; many persons of a certain age lose their teeth, but her loss seemed so sudden. There are false teeth to be had, and she acquired them. Then her hair fell out, handfuls at a time, her beautiful bronzy hair. There are wigs to be bought, so she wore another woman's hair. Then her heart weakened. Her hands shook. She lost her balance and fell constantly if I didn't hold onto her; she garbled her words; and worst of all, her voice.…"

The Count erupts in sobs, his face in his hands. Constanze lays her hand once again on his sword arm and pats it. Some time goes by.

"I am an old military man, my dear. Weeping is not encouraged among our officers and men, but there are times when there is weeping—even in the military, because we need to. I am not ashamed to weep before you now. The paramount rule for an officer is this: you take care of your men. Life is harsh, and deadly—or worse—on the battlefield. You do not desert those in your charge, and I have never done so. Nor did I desert MariLise, even when her voice became like that of a beast, her mind slipped away, and she began to smell like a...."

Constanze leans further forward, and murmurs,

"You are a good and a great man, dear Count. You have answered every call. But tell me, if you will, could the doctors not help the poor Countess? Did they have nothing to say about her illness?"

"We consulted several doctors; they told me nothing but terrible news: that her heart, kidneys, liver, and brain were in a state of progressive and irreversible deterioration. There was nothing to be done."

Constanze sits up straight in her chair during this last speech, eyes wide, face frozen in shock.

"All those terrible symptoms," she whispered, "I heard a similar diagnosis only yesterday. But it was for Herr Hambacher, not the Countess. Those words, so close, I swear! Is there some sort of plague happening here?"

"Hambacher? I thought he died of a heart attack *in media res* with a certain woman! Pardon my frankness, dear lady. Ah, perhaps...."

"Did Herr Hambacher have a connection to the Countess at all?"

"Yes, actually. Hambacher paid the salary of one of our singers, indeed that 'certain woman,' the one who bolted. And MariLise's family had substantial interests in mines and minerals. Hambacher invested in this business at her invitation, and it was arranged for him to get a steep discount on lead, and mercury sulfide, I believe, for his *Geschmink* compounding business. You know, *rouge et blanc*? It's such an obsession for women here. As my wife's beauty faded away she insisted on using more and more of his products, and he of course allowed her to take whatever she thought she needed, gratis. It was too much for my taste, but I think perhaps she knew more about her decay than I thought she did, and wanted to hide herself. Not only in the Estates Box, but behind an ever-thickening mask of paint. I much prefer ladies who look cultivate a more natural look, like you, if I may say so, Frau Mozart."

Frau Mozart continues to stare into the face of Mozart's patron, Count Franz Anton Nostic, her fingers over her lips.

"Have I said something too forward, Madame? Have I offended in some way? What is the matter with you?"

   "Lead. For white. And cinnabar, for red." she whispers to herself.

   "What about them, Frau Mozart? What about them?"

   "They're poison. Slow poison."

Disinherited

Bertramka Villa, October 27 and 28, 1787

Ah le membra fermar più non sò

Lorenzo Da Ponte and Giacomo Casanova, having rescued Mozart from the murderous designs of Count Nostic, observe that the composer is shaking like a leaf and turning blue around the lips. They bundle him in their own outer garments, hail a carriage and take him over the bridge toward Bertramka. On the journey the two Venetians warm the little man with their own larger bodies, at great personal cost. They will both become ill.

Wolfgang having also caught a chill and a mortal fright from his misadventures the previous night, is filled with gratitude toward his rescuers and for the tender care provided by Josepha and Constanze. They have wrapped him in shawls, heated up warming pans, plied him with strong drinks, and put him to bed with a nice wife to keep him company. His color and good spirits return, but the horror of near death has entered into his bones and he cannot stop trembling.

The three of them are now in the music room crowding close to the stove. Mozart is sitting on the floor, trying to disguise his shaking by teasing Josepha's Pomeranian dog with treats from his half-eaten lunch and talking to it in a stream of nonsense. Nobody is fooled for an instant, including the dog.

"I just received a long letter from my cousin Colomba in Salzburg, you remember her of course? One paragraph of her letter contains some news that concerns you both," says Josepha, pouring coffee for her friends. "I'm afraid it's not exactly pleasant news. Of course, if you would rather defer hearing it until after opening night, I am sure it can wait. Or perhaps you want to be able to respond to this news as soon as possible."

"Frankly," says Wolfgang, "after what I have been through recently, nothing will ever perturb me again. And don't worry about opening night, dear Madame," "You have lifted the entire cast, kicking and screaming, into a state of high energy and readiness. I am so grateful you consented to step in and show them how it's done."

"And I am equally grateful for yet another aria, springing full-formed from your pen—or the Head of Zeus! It seems I must confront all my demons when I sing it, and yet not let them get the better of me. It is a joyful and a daunting task I face."

"Have no fear, dear Josepha! When the music inhabits us, we will forget all our recent shocks, including any silly tittle-tattle from the thrice-damned Duchy of Salzburg. In other words, go ahead and read."

"My cousin has continued her friendship with your sister, since we all first met in Salzburg ten years ago. They have corresponded and visited each other after Nannerl married and moved to St. Gilgen. She writes that she has had a letter from your sister, Frau von Berchtold that is, in which she mentions that her father's will has been read, and that his entire fortune has been settled on her. Forgive me, but there seems to have been quite a large sum of money involved."

Silence.

Mozart sits absently stroking the dog, who has stopped frisking and become very still.

"How large a sum?" says Constanze.

"Close to eight thousand *Gulden*, apparently."

Another longer silence ensues. Finally, Mozart speaks.

"He sold it all. Our childhood earnings. All of it. Trunks and cabinets and wardrobes stuffed full…and he sold it and gave the money to the one who has no need of it." Mozart rises and goes to sit beside his wife, who has turned very pale. She holds his hands. He is trembling all over.

"My little sword, the medals, the jewels, the snuff boxes, the watches, the trinkets, all the gifts handed to us by all those royal and noble hands, that would not soil themselves to reach further into their pockets and pay us in hard cash. Half the money belongs to Nannerl, of course. But the other half…."

"And we are so deep in debt, too," says Constanze. "I was hoping for a bequest from Salzburg so we could begin to honor those debts. Now we may never…."

"Ach! Dammit to hell! That devil of a man comes back from beyond the grave to punish me yet again! Is he never done with his self- righteous condemnations of me? What crime did I ever do that he persecutes me so? Am I such a libertine? No! Here's what I did! I moved to Vienna, I shopped myself to the Imperial Court, I found patrons, I worked my ass off leading a freelance life, I fell in love, I got married! All these nefarious deeds I did, in the teeth of his eternal disapproval! What in fucking hell did he want from me? To stay in Salzburg under his eye, under his thumb, doing shitwork for Colloredo all my life? To obey his smallest wish, as my poor sister has done?

"My sad miserable wretch of a sister did his bidding like a galley slave! She stopped seeing the man she loved and married dear Papa's choice, that rich dumb ox Berchtold. She raised his insolent brats and ran his establishment, a house so damp and mildewed that her clavier rotted away under her fingers. Then, having not abased herself *quite* enough— When Papa demanded it, she gave him her first-born son—*little Leopold*, of course!—to raise as he saw fit in Salzburg, because Papa thought he could create another infant prodigy to drag around Europe and steal money from! My poor deluded sister! Her performing career gone, her composing gifts quashed, her marriage loveless, her mind rotting away just like her clavier, for lack of stimulation."

"Perhaps," says Constanze, "she might still offer us your half, or some slice of it, after all. If you wrote and told her what our situation is, she would soften towards you and do it. She doesn't need the money, and now that your Papa is gone she might be amenable...."

"She'll *never*! He rules over her from the grave, from the lowest depths of hell, where I am certain he is now dining on roast pheasant with Satan. How I hate him! How I will always hate him. He has *ruined my life*!"

Shaking and sobbing, Wolfgang beats his knees with his fists.

Josepha draws her chair nearer the couple.

"My poor dears, my heart aches to see you in such pain. What a blessing it is, dear Wolfgang, that you left home and became your own man, a man with such splendid gifts to give the world. Please let me help you if I can. You are always welcome here, welcome to come live at Bertramka to set yourselves up in Prague and start over, if your situation in Vienna becomes too dire. I promise to assist you in every endeavor. Forget family tribulations! Everybody loves you here! Think of our wonderful musical people, our superb orchestra, our lovely countryside, our fine and venerable city."

"Not to mention the excellent jail," says Mozart, laughing through tears. "I *do* think about it, Madame, I weigh it often in my heart. But my heart keeps telling me that while I love Prague immeasurably, Vienna is the center of the Empire, and I must be in the center.

"I don't know right now what to do, except— I must work twice as hard and allow my dear wife once again to scrimp and save every penny. She is such a good manager, but money has no hold on my mind. Even so, the debt we owe our friends and patrons—it haunts me! I promise though, if we are turned out into the street in Vienna, we will creep like beggars to your door. But God, I wish I were free. And now I will never be free."

"I think you are wrong, Wolfgang. Listen," says Josepha, taking his hand.

"You. And I. You and I have suffered terrible betrayals by those who loved and understood us best, and whom we loved best—in spite of everything. You and I feel a blazing rage and deep hurt. But I know this present agony will not last. I know that after this opera is sung and the curtain rolls down, I will be free. And you too will be free."

Mozart extends his other hand to Constanze.

"Look," she says. "The trembling has stopped."

All three bow their heads close together and weep quietly. The dog curls up and lays his silken and sympathetic head on their feet.

In quali eccesi, o Numi, in quai misfatti orribili tremendi, è avvolto it sciagurato! Ah no! non puote tardar l'ira del cielo, la giustizia tardar. Sentir già parmi la fatale saetta, che gli piomba sul capo! Aperto veggio il baratro mortal!Misera Elvira! Che contrasto d'affetti in sen ti nasce! Perchè questi sospiri? E quest'ambascie?

Mi tradì quell'alma ingrata,
Infelice, o Dio, mi fa!
Ma tradita e abbandonata
Provo ancor per lui pietà.
Quando sento il mio tormento
Di vendetta il cor favella,
Ma se guardo il suo cimento,
Palpitando il cor mi va.

In what excesses, o Gods, in what horrible dreadful crimes is this wretched man involved! Ah, no! The wrath of heaven and justice cannot wait! I think I can hear the fatal thunderbolt, that will fall on his head! I see hell's abyss yawning open! Pitiful Elvira! What a mix of feelings arise in your heart! Why these sighs? And these sorrows?

He betrayed me, that ungrateful soul
He made me, O God, so miserable!
But betrayed and abandoned
I still feel pity for him.
When I feel my torment
My heart speaks of vendetta,
But if I see his ordeal,
My heart goes throbbing

Text by Lorenzo Da Ponte

Opening Night

The Nostic National Theater, October 29, 1787

Dammi la mano in pegna

Opening Night of *Don Giovanni* is a total triumph. Each performer brings his or her personal swarm of demons to the performance, and each strives to exorcise them before of a cloud of witnesses, who have brought demons of their own into the Theater. Everyone present feels in their bones that something incomprehensible is happening to them. Demons and imps and ghosts leave their trembling bodies and fly free around the theater so long as the music sounds. All the cruelty and violence and lies and betrayals they have committed or suffered are revealed for the hellish horrors that they are, looming over them and then seeming to dissolve and disappear through the roof during the final *stretto* of the finale. An eerie silence reigns.

Then the thunder begins. The audience is stamping, clapping, and shrieking in a frenzy of released emotion, shaking the entire building. They and the exhausted performers feel free and joyful and renewed. Are their demons truly cast out forever? Or are they just lying in wait in the dark outside?

Luigi Bassi, having emitted his last cry of agony as Don Giovanni, and having been dragged down to hell, or down to the trap room under the stage, by the chorus dressed in scarlet and black demon costumes, stands transfixed, as if turned to stone. The choral demons still crowd around him, laughing and weeping and congratulating him and themselves. The three trombonists consigned to the trap room join the throng, thumping Bassi on the shoulders and bellowing "bravo!" But Bassi pays no attention. He is staring at another one who is there, standing a little aside; a figure dressed in black.

He recognizes this apparition, and scrambles backward away from it, his eyes wild, his mouth screaming soundlessly. The figure advances, his hand held out. Bassi falls to his knees, silently weeping. The dark figure speaks in a low voice.

"Give me your hand."

Bassi prostrates himself sobbing and pounding his head on the floorboards. Minutes pass as the demons and brass players silently encircle the standing figure and the groveling young man.

Finally, the dark figure bends down and clasps the singer's hand, helping him rise. It wraps its cloak around him and leads him away, as the audience is heard still rhythmically clapping and calling out his name, yowling with increasing insistence. The two are seen on the street walking slowly, heads lowered, with their arms around each other, in the direction of the Police House.

Mozart Gets Out of Jail Free

Bertramka October 30, 1787

Questo è il fin

"I've been such a jackass! I want to apologize to you all," says Mozart, springing up from his chair. Josepha and František Dušek, Constanze Mozart and Count Christian Clam-Gallas are once again lounging in the music room in the hour just before dawn. They have talked over the wonders of the evening's performance, drunk the good wines of South Bohemia, and now they sit in silent communion gazing at the fire in the sweet porcelain stove that is warming them all.

"Apologies are not necessary after such a triumphant achievement as tonight's, surely, Mozart," says the Count.

"Oh yesyesyes they *are*! Let me apologize! I need to! I have been clowning and pranking and what's worse, cruelly crushing and humiliating so many people, people whom I love as I love my life. You, dear and irreplaceable Dušeks. My wife. My heroic cast. Bassi, who wanted nothing more than a big aria, which I denied him out of sheer meanness. And worse, I mocked and derided her who can no longer hear me begging her pardon.

"I was unspeakably rude to Kretènček, our good Chief of Police. I made fun of Pospíšil's name too, and he my most loyal fan. I pranked old Casanova, who turned around and saved my life at midnight on the docks. And my dear Da Ponte too. Jackass is too mild a word for how I've been behaving. Help me out here."

"Jerk?" murmurs Constanze.

"Agreed."

"Boor?" says František.

"Accepted."

"A soul in pain?" says Josepha.

"No excuses!" Mozart answers. "I deserve censure from you all."

"Really not," says Josepha. Your demons, or at least this most recent set anyway, are laid to rest. You wrote a demonic masterpiece. You've been horribly betrayed by him whom you both loved and hated, and you are now quit of that hate and free to love whatever was good about him. You have repented of your ill-use of your colleagues and patrons and your jailers. You have asked forgiveness from us for your wrongdoings. You are free to go on, as I am free—thanks to you and Constanze!—to go onto a stage and sing the role, and the mighty heart-scorching *scena* you wrote for me. Singing it last night was a revelation to me, as I struggle to come to terms with my feelings. So, we around this fire, and I especially, forgive you your sins, bless you, and thank you from the depths of my heart."

A long silence follows.

A servant enters and announces the Chief of Prague Police Kretènček and Constable Pospíšil.

"Speak of the police and they appear!" says everyone. And they do.

"Ladies, gentlemen! First, Sir Mozart, what an opera! Funny and scary and true all at once! Yes, of course we heard it! We were there providing extra security and crowd control, and we all think *Don Giovanni* is your best one yet! We are all humming that 'Latchkey la mano' duet all night long."

"Let us not speak of keys this evening, if you please," says Josepha. "We have spent fruitless hours thinking about keys, and we are forever done with them. To what do we owe this early visit, Mr. Chief? I hope there is nothing amiss?"

"Well, Madame, and by the way, bravo for every note, but let me get to the point. Mr. Bassi, who sang so beautifully last night, came to the Police House directly after the show, without never even taking a curtain call, before the noise and applause had died down and the crowd had dispersed. He was accompanied by His Excellency Count Nostic. They were sitting together waiting for me when I arrived.

"Bassi confessed to the killing of Countess Nostic, which both he and the Count seem to think was tragic but entirely accidental and having something to do with Bassi imagining he needed to kill Mozart with a Tyrolean air rifle which misfired in the Theater where she also was."

"Wait, what? Somebody *else* was going to kill me? With a rifle?" shouts Mozart."

"Hush, I'll explain later, if you can't work it out for yourself," says Constanze.

"Then, if I may," continues the Chief, "the Count confessed that he too had tried to kill Mozart with his saber but was dissuaded from doing so by Madame Mozart.

"Of course, all of us policemen got very angry, hearing they had both tried to kill Mozart, and several officers wanted to throw them both into the dungeon and beat them up good and properly. But we thought better of that and decided we should consult with you before we did it. We are still willing, though. I stopped by on my way to let the Constable know, and he insisted on coming along. He says he has something to return to Mr. Mozart, which he will now do."

"It's the first page of your sketch of 'Bella mia flame' you wrote that night before I arrested you," says Pospíšil. "It was lying in a dark corner on the floor of the Police House. Confiscated as evidence, was my guess, and dropped by accident, but it seems nobody cared much about it. I picked it up and thought to keep it as a souvenir, but on second thought I decided that would not be right. Here it is, I'm sorry; it has been wonderful to look at it every day this whole month, but it belongs to you."

Pospíšil hands the sheet over to Mozart. Mozart hands it over to Josepha, who hands it back to him.

"Sign it," she says. Mozart finds a pen and ink, signs his name and the place and date, and returns it to Josepha.

"Here you are, my good man, it is yours to keep forever," says the diva, giving it again to the Constable, who bursts into tears. Mozart embraces him heartily. Constanze and Kretènček are moved to join them in a hug *a quatre*.

"I've got to go there, now," says Constanze at last, "I mean the Police House. I am a witness and I want to give a statement in support of both Bassi and Nostic. May I go back across the river with you, dear Chief?"

"Yes, of course, dearest Madame Mozart."

"And I'll go too! I have some things I want to say!" shouts the famous genius.

"No, darling," says Constanze, "You are going to stay here. I have some even more important things to say to the police and to Bassi and Count Nostic. I believe I have solved the mystery of the Death of Herr Hambacher as well.

"What!!" says the entire ensemble. "Tell! Tell!"

"If I may delay a moment, Chief, I will tell. It won't take long. It is as plain as the noses on our faces. Why didn't we see it? Namely: mercury and lead. Red and white. The late Herr Hambacher compounded these colors for all your high-class ladies and theater folk to wear. He worked day after day, grinding the lead and cinnabar in a small back room, breathing the dust, slowly poisoning himself. I didn't think about it until the good Count Nostic mentioned his wife's ongoing illness, which produced the same symptoms as Herr Hambacher had. He told me about his poor wife's sufferings in almost the same words that appeared in the coroner's final report on Herr Hambacher's demise. Progressive organ deterioration and failure and so on. And...came the dawn!"

"We killed him," murmurs Josepha. "We women of Prague, and our painted masquerade. We did it, all of us. But it seems now that we women also may pay dearly...."

"Since all Prague ladies and performers wear extravagant makeup," says Constanze, "I don't quite see why only Countess Nostic seemed to be so vulnerable to its effects; but perhaps her interest in mines and minerals brought her into more than usual contact with the poisons. Or perhaps her advanced age may have hastened her decline. Others may resist the poison longer and not become ill, but who knows?

"But! if *I* were living here (and I soon may be!) I would agitate in every square for a change in the fashion. I hear that fine ladies are spurning the heavy paint in London, preferring the more natural look; we would be well advised to follow their good example in Prague, if we want to stop killing ourselves, and others. And now I must be off to set a few things right on the other side of the river."

Josepha caught Constanze's hand as she moved toward the door.

"Thank you," she whispered.

"No murders at all in this tale. Close, but not one murder, did I mention that?"

"It's what you did not mention that I am thanking you for."

After embracing her hostess, Constanze vanished with her police escort.

"Why wouldn't she let me go with her?" says Mozart.

"Because, dear Mozart," says Josepha, "Bassi confessed his misdeed to her. His sad confidence forged a strong bond of trust and friendship between them now. Your presence would not be desirable, do you understand?"

"How do you know he confessed to her? She told me she had dropped him."

"She had. She told me the whole sad story while you were busy writing the overture. Young Bassi begged her to see him again; he needed to tell her what he had planned to do, and what he had done. She heard his terrible tale sympathetically, even the part about wanting to kill you and buying a gun and bullets. Their little flirtation had fizzled, only to be replaced by something deeper: a true friendship. Do you object to that, since it was his confession that saved your jackass's skin?"

"No, I don't object any more. Constanze is magnificent. I love her. I trust her. My darling will never betray me. And I love you too, Josepha. I don't know what games you wondrous women have been up to, but I'm indebted to you both—among many, many others—for bringing all this murder nonsense to a close and saving me from Bassi, Nostic, Papa, and, incidentally, from myself."

"Well said, beloved friend. Because you too must own some part in Bassi's tragic killing of the Countess, must you not? You mocked the poor boy in front of everyone; he was so humiliated that he went and got a gun to shoot you with. God help us; it seems that we are all of us entangled in this poisoned web of hurting and killing, accidentally or purposefully, in this happy and unhappy hour. I pray that henceforth we always readily repent, beg forgiveness, and forgive, put aside our grievances—and grieve!—that we might lay our demons to rest. In so doing, we might transform that foul and fatal web into a golden net of fellowship, patience, understanding and love. But can we do it? Who can tell what the future might bring?"

"Dear lady," says Mozart, "You have spoken a prayer and a poem. I can only say '*Ah, tutti contenti saremo così!*'"

Appendix I

Character Notes

I callously bent a lot of truths about the historic persons who appear in this book to suit my needs. I feel that, since the many Mozart hagiographies also played fast and loose with the truth about the great man and his circle, there is a precedent for my doing it too. I hereby unbend some truths to the best of my knowledge, with apologies to all whom I have maligned.

Johannes Chrysostomus Wolfganus Theophilus Mozart (1756–1791), aka Amadeo Wolfgano Mozart, or Wolfgang Gottlieb Mozart, Amadé Mozart, and many other variations on his baptismal name, was a prodigal and prodigious composer of over 600 musical works (of which 22 were operas), in addition to being virtuoso performer on keyboard instruments and viola. He enjoyed theater, dancing, flirting, playing billiards and practical jokes, and talking in rhymes. It is true that he rode a horse for exercise, smoked a pipe, and kept dogs and singing birds. Also true, he really was a crack shot with the airgun. I believe he managed to be mostly happy, despite the many setbacks and hardships in his short but incredibly rich and productive life.

Giacomo Girolamo Casanova. Justly christened "a true Enlightenment polymath," the several-times-larger-than life Casanova led a life of perpetual adventure, if half the tales are true. He was, at various times, a professional gambler, violinist, astrologer, amateur physician, a master Freemason, mathematician, duelist, playwright, author, numerologist, prisoner, alchemist, foreign emissary, tireless traveler, and memoirist (12 volumes!!). In addition, he was the inventor and, to this day the most notorious practitioner of the Love Bomb (120 recorded love affairs in his magnificent but unfinished autobiography!). A friend of Lorenzo Da Ponte. He may or may not have met Mozart.

Teresa Saporiti, one of the two singing Saporiti sisters in Bondini's troupe, the creator of the role of Donna Anna. She also sang the role of the Countess in the Prague production *Figaro*. She sang all over Europe and composed several arias. Saporiti retired to her hometown of Milan, and held musical salons in her house, in the course of which Giuseppe Verdi presented some of his music. She died, as the Prague fortune-teller predicted, at the age of 106.

Caterina Saporiti Bondini sang the roles of Susanna and Zerlina in the Prague premieres. She married the head of the opera troupe Pasquale Bondini and produced five little Bondinis, probably continuing to sing with the company during her pregnancies, as was the custom. Or the necessity.

Luigi Bassi created the roles of Count Alamaviva and Don Giovanni. He did, as my fictitious Mozart predicted, lose his voice early, and became known for performing comprimario parts, including Papageno in Mozart's *Die Zauberflöte*. In later life he sang exclusively liturgical repertoire.

Josepha Dušek. Some true facts about the great diva were altered to make a better tale, so I will now correct them. Josepha's beloved father Anton Adalbert Hambacher died when she was a young girl, and probably did not do any of the dissolute acts I have attributed to him. Josepha and her husband František produced three children, who formed a singing trio and toured around Europe. Josepha had a long and remarkable concert career; although upon her husband's death she withdrew from performing, becoming more and more impoverished until her death in 1824, as foreseen by my fictitious Prague fortune-teller. She never sang the role of Donna Elvira.

Countess Maria Elisabeth von Nostic. All the evidence points to the Countess as the ringleader of a noblewomen's conspiracy to prevent the presentation of *Le Nozze di Figaro* for the honeymooning royals. She was the highest-ranking noble in Prague, the de facto Queen of the city, who felt no qualms about yelling *"ho vinto"* at Mozart from her box in the theater, and she actually did so. Count Leopold Le Noble von Edlersberg arrived in Prague in the nick of time to intervene on Mozart's behalf, and the *Figaro* performance went on. The composer claimed to have been amused at being screamed at in public by the Countess, and perhaps he was.

Caterina Micelli. In Alfred Meissner's highly imaginative—if not totally fictitious—reconstruction of a picnic at Bertramka, Micelli's mamma claimed to have been three times to the fortune-teller to have her daughter's cards read. Three times the prophetess had predicted that Caterina would soon have a position as a chamber singer at a royal court. Caterina reportedly clapped both her hands over her mamma's mouth and pooh-poohed all such prophecies. It is not known whether the cards spoke the truth, but it was fun to imagine that Micelli lived out her mamma's dream and skedaddled in the direction of the nearest royalty before the premiere of *Don Giovanni*. Of course she did not skedaddle, but performed the role of Donna Elvira in the world premiere in Prague.

Constanze Mozart and her sisters. Mozart's wife and three sisters-in-law were all trained sopranos. Their father, Franz Fridolin Weber, was, by several accounts, a contrabass player, a singer, a prompter in the theater and a music copyist. First based in Mannheim, Germany, the family moved twice to follow the eldest daughter's engagements, which supported the entire family; first to Munich, and finally to Vienna.

The eldest sister, Aloysia, enjoyed a significant international career; the second eldest, Josepha Weber, was a noted singer who created the role of the Queen of the Night in *The Magic Flute*. Constanze, married to Mozart, never worked as a professional singer, although she sang the difficult solos in her husband's Great Mass in C minor in Salzburg in 1783. The youngest sister, Sophie, performed for a few seasons at the Burgtheater in Vienna.

Mozart flirted with all the Weber sisters, but Aloysia was his first serious crush. He loved her singing and her incredible range, and wrote five concert arias for her (including "Popolo di Tessaglia," which features a G above high

C). Aloysia appeared in Mozart's operas as Madame Herz, Konstanze, Donna Anna, and Sesto, despite having icily refused his offer of marriage. The sensitive young composer, deeply wounded upon being rebuffed, was purported to have said, or sung: "Whoever doesn't want me can kiss my ass," and married Constanze instead.

Constanze settled down to domestic duties and the production of many Mozart offspring (only two of whom survived to adulthood), singing as a gifted amateur, and encouraging her husband to write Baroque counterpoint, for which she had a particular liking.

After Mozart's death, Constanze set about tidying up his legacy. She made sure her late husband's works were legitimately published. She presented a series of profitable concerts in his memory and extracted a widow's pension from the Emperor. She shared her reminiscences with two authors working on Mozart biographies. She married again in 1809, to the author of the second biography, the Danish diplomat Georg Nikolaus von Nissen. She oversaw publication of this book in 1828, after Nissen's death.

Josepha Weber also had stratospheric high notes, but was only required to ascend to a mere F above high C when she created the role of Queen of the Night in the Theater an der Wien where she reigned as prima donna. She married twice, retired, and lived her entire adult life in Vienna.

Sophie, the baby of the family, was described by Mozart as "feather-brained," is now best known for her heart-rending descriptions of the composer's last days: how she and Constanze sewed him a quilted bed jacket that could be put on from the front, because the poor man was so swollen up he could not turn over in bed; and how she, Sophie, stampeded around town to summon her mother and the attending physician to the sickroom when Mozart took a turn for the worse. The good doctor, reluctant to leave the theater where he was watching a play, showed up after the final curtain, and prescribed the cold poultices which put his patient into a coma from which he never emerged. According to Sophie anyway.

There are several gruesome and wildly contradictory commentaries about Mozart's last hours, delivered by various witnesses who may or may not have been there; by the sisters (who were indeed there), and by Mozart's assistant Franz Xaver Süssmayr (probably there). Efforts were made to make these witness stories as pathetic as possible, in order to stir the hearts of patrons, publishers, fans, biographers, and other sources of future income for the widow of the great man.

When Sophie's husband died, she moved in with Constanze, now twice widowed and living in Salzburg. When Aloysia was also widowed, she joined her two sisters, and the three kept house together until the end.

Lorenzo Da Ponte. This man did so many things, became so many things, and said so many things, both true and untrue! Where to begin? Poet, polyglot, orator, charmer of women, scholar, impresario; and, as one writer described him, a "professional insolvent."

However, unlike his friend and fellow-Venetian Casanova, Da Ponte was never in jail. But he could have been.

I am going to tell you some of his story in reverse order, since he spent the better part (in both senses) of his life in the United States. He arrived on our shores in 1805, fleeing London and his creditors with his new wife, Nancy. London was just one of the many major European cities from which he was forced to decamp.

In America Da Ponte labored for a brief time as a greengrocer, then as a bookseller, and an Italian tutor. He was "discovered" by Clement Clark Moore (of "'Twas the Night Before Christmas" fame) and became a literary lion in New York society. He founded the Italian department at Columbia University, while also acting as an impresario, bringing the brightest European stars (Malibran! García!) to New York. He raised funds for America's first real Opera House in 1833, when he was 89 years of age.

Occasionally, stories of his shady sexual and financial past drifted across the Atlantic, but these sordid tales from decadent Europe did not seem to bother his American friends and students very much. They loved him.

Da Ponte, equally in love with his new country, made a fresh start: giving up his libertine ways, settling down with his adored wife and siring a quartet of charming and talented children. His financial woes followed him, however, to the end of his days. He died in 1838, and his funeral overflowed with mourners. And creditors.

In 1783 Da Ponte arrived in Vienna after a peripatetic failed job search.

With nothing but his wits and a letter of introduction to the composer Salieri, he wangled himself the job of Imperial Poet to the Court of Joseph II. The Emperor remained steadfastly loyal to Da Ponte until the day he banished him from Vienna in 1790.

He wangled a patron also, the building magnate Raimund Wetzlar von Plankenstern, who was also a patron of Mozart's. In his memoirs, Da Ponte claims that Mozart begged him on bended knee for a libretto. But he claims a lot of things in his memoirs. Howsoever their collaboration began, it produced three sublime operas.

In 1773, Da Ponte, who was of Jewish origin, was ordained as an Abbate in the Catholic Church. He continued to reside in a Venetian brothel with his lady friend, with whom he had two children. Accused of organizing all sorts of bawdy entertainments in the brothel, he was tried on morals charges and banished from Venice in 1779.

In 1749, the gifted child Emanuel Conegliano was born in Ceneda, in the Republic of Venice. He attended the Ceneda seminary and was baptized Lorenzo Da Ponte by the presiding Bishop. He taught at the Seminary before moving into the city of Venice and beginning his life of dissipation, bad business deals, immortal librettos, and American successes.

Count Franz Anton von Nostic. After a distinguished military career in the Wars of Austrian Succession, Nostic became the presiding officer of the Gubernium, a congress of elites performing both executive and judicial duties in the Bohemian Lands. He was the de facto king of Bohemia and the leading patron of the literary and theatrical arts. Nostic built the magnificent Nostic National Theater (later called the National Theater. It is still in use today, and called The Estates Theater) at his personal expense. He wanted to make his theater available to all social classes and encouraged productions in Czech as well as German. He hired Pasquale Bondini to bring Italian opera to Prague, holding the opinion that opera productions, being incomprehensible, provided the perfect background noise for idling, flirting, eating, and talking over the performances. I think he underestimated the music lovers of Prague, at least where Mozart was concerned.

Death by Beauty Products. Women—and men too—have been putting toxic substances on their faces for millennia. Lead, arsenic and mercury, belladonna, Botox, Parabens, Phthalates, coal tar, you name it! If it makes you look fashionable, you put it on. Yes, to this day we are still putting it on.

Elizabeth I of England and Ireland, born in 1533, may have applied a lead/vinegar concoction called "ceruse" to whiten and smooth out her pockmarked skin. Ceruse causes skin damage, forcing the user to increase the coverage over time to cover it up. Ladies in the 18th century were still painting themselves with this stuff before they switched to arsenic in the 19th. They also applied Vermillion, containing mercury sulfide, to their cheeks and lips.

The poster child for death by beauty products—and one of my inspirations for this book—is Maria Coventry, Countess of Coventry (born in 1732), a woman so drop-dead gorgeous she had to hire bodyguards to keep her adoring fans from mobbing her when she went out. She set the English fashion for a dead-white face and heavily rouged cheeks, refusing to give up her beauty regime even though her husband hated it.

Gorgeous Maria did drop dead, probably of lead poisoning, at the age of 27. It is said that she was thickly made-up in lead-white and rouge to receive visitors as she lay dying.

Please check the ingredient lists on your beauty products. If there is a list, that is. There are some really nasty things in there.

Appendix II

Chapter Headings Translated

The Italian phrases in the chapter headings are all, with one exception, quotes from Da Ponte's libretto for Don Giovanni.

E aperto a tutti quanti, viva la libertà.
(It's open to everyone, long live liberty.)

Il padre? Lascia, o cara, la rimembranza amara!
(Your father? O dear, put aside that bitter memory!).

Si eccelente è'l vostro cuoco, che lo volli anch'io provar
(Your chef is so excellent that I wanted to taste it too.)

Ehi, cafè! Ciocolatte!
(Hey, Coffee! Chocolate!)

Regina, io vado ad ubbidirti!
(Queen, I am going to obey you!)

Ah! Dov'è il perfido? Dov'è l'indegno? Tutto il mio sdegno sfogar io vo.
(Ah! Where is the wicked man? Where is the wretch? I want to vent all my indignation.)

E tutto amore; chi a una sola è fedele, verso l'altre è crudele.
(Love is everything; whoever is faithful to one only, is cruel towards the others.)

Là ci darem la mano
(There we will join hands)

Capisco, briconcella! Hai timor Ch'io comprenda com'è tra voi passata la faccenda.
(I get it, you little rascal! You're afraid that I understand what went on between you.)

Non voglio più servir, no no no no no
(I don't want to serve any more, no no no no no no)

Deh vieni alla finestra
(O come to the window)

Sarete sempre mio? Sempre!
(Will you be mine forever? Forever!)

Lasciala, indegno, battiti meco!
(Let her go, you wretch, fight with me!)

E un orribile tempesta minacciando, o Dio, mi va!
(And a horrible storm is threatening me, o God!)

Finch'han dal vino
(As long as they have some wine)

Ah, taci, ingiusto core!
(Ah be silent, unjust heart!)

Madamina, il catologo è questo
(Little lady, this is the catalogue)

Ah, chi mi dice mai quell' barbaro dov'è?
(Ah, who can tell me where that barbarian is?)

Vedrai, carino
(You'll see, dearie)

Di rider finirai pria dell'aurora!
(You'll finish laughing before dawn!)

Dalla sua Pace la mia dipende
(My peace depends on hers)

Ah le membra fermar più non so
(Ah I can't stop my limbs from shaking)

Dammi la mano in pegna
(Give me your hand as a pledge)

Questo è il fin
(This is the end)

End Note

Many Thanks to my sensitive and perceptive readers and sage advisors: Susan Davenny Wyner, Jaylyn Olivo, Robert Wexelblatt, Lloyd Schwartz, Jan Swafford, and Jim Haber! Thanks to my sister Ellen, who is always generous with technical advice. Thanks to my copy editor, soprano/conductor Danica Buckley, who loves the Oxford comma and rejoices in semicolons.

www.ingramcontent.com/pod-product-compliance
Lightning Source LLC
Chambersburg PA
CBHW070934250626
47159CB00009B/3241